A Perfectly Good Man
A Coffee and Donuts Book

Amanda Hamm

ISBN: 978-1-943598-97-7

Also by Amanda Hamm

Sofie Waits (Coffee and Donuts #2)

Said and Unsaid (Coffee and Donuts #1)

The Christmas Project (Stories From Hartford #4)

Collecting Zebras (Stories From Hartford #3)

Jealousy & Yams (Stories From Hartford #2)

Andrew's Key (Stories From Hartford #1)

The 4th Floor Lounge

Meet Cute: 5 Romantic Short Stories

Weathering Evan

1

I lay in bed Sunday morning trying to decide if I felt any different. My room looked exactly the same. The pink comforter I'd had since I was a kid was folded up at my feet. It wasn't necessary in June. A poster of optical illusions hung on the otherwise blank white walls.

Tyler called while I was still sitting on the edge of the bed, trying to get myself all the way up. He always called to wish me a good day and always sounded amused by my unintelligible thoughts for his. I had oatmeal for breakfast, which was boring and didn't feel or taste different. When I finished my shower and began to look for something to wear, I knew I was getting close to something different. It wasn't the dress with the green and white flowers. I'd had that for years. It wasn't the tan sandals. Scuff marks on the fronts said they weren't different.

I flipped on my hairdryer and nothing happened. A few quick knocks against my palm brought it to life. I had to tie my hair back for work so I liked seeing it around my face and shoulders. But I wore it down nearly every Sunday so that wasn't different. I'd recently lightened it to a medium blond. After three weeks, I was completely used to it. I looked in the mirror and saw nothing different.

The ring was different. A white gold circle sat next to the sink looking insignificant. I picked it up and slipped it onto the ring finger of my left hand. Today I was engaged. Tyler had proposed less than twelve hours ago. The ring definitely felt different on my finger.

When guys proposed in books or movies, they usually made romantic speeches about love and building a life together. Tyler had said, "I've been thinking, and I want to ask you to marry me."

That wasn't even a question. Of course, I had said, "Okay," which wasn't yes either. I wondered if the queasy feeling in my stomach was because we hadn't followed the script. I'd always been very practical and rarely sentimental though. And he'd looked so relieved. I guessed the unsettled feeling was simply the newness of being engaged. It would surely dissipate after I'd had a chance to get used to the idea.

I fought back a yawn as I got in my car to drive to church. I preferred to go to the later mass when I didn't have to work, but Tyler always went to the early service at his church. I had to go early, too, if I wanted to see him afterwards.

The choir began a prelude as I entered Sacred Heart. I found an empty pew and sat near the middle of it. My mom always grumbled about people who came early and plopped themselves on the end of a row for others to climb over. She'd once said that aisle seats should be reserved for those with small children or prostate problems.

I liked to know what songs we were going to sing ahead of time. It was a habit I'd had since I was a little girl and first figured out what the numbers meant. I opened a hymnal and flipped through the pages to find the first song. Not one of my favorites. I turned a few pages to find the next one.

Movement to my left caused me to look up. Good morning was on my lips to greet whomever was joining me in the pew. The pleasantry faded away in surprise as I recognized the man.

"This seat taken?" he whispered.

I shook my head. "What are you doing here?" I didn't mean to sound rude, only confused. He always went to the church next door with Tyler.

He simply smiled and shrugged as though he didn't know what he was doing there either.

I was holding the hymnal on my lap with my left hand, and it was covering the ring. I was nervous about telling people, but I'd thought at least John Myrie would hear the news from Tyler. Now I wasn't so sure. John was Tyler's best friend so he probably knew he was going to ask me. But did he know I'd said yes?

Or rather, did he know I'd said okay?

I checked the other song numbers slowly, keeping the hymnal over my hand as long as I could. John sat quietly next to me with his hands folded in his lap. He might have been praying. I wanted to see if his eyes were closed, but if they weren't he'd see me looking.

If I could hide the ring at least until the mass started, it would be harder for him to say anything. I burrowed my left hand against my stomach as I leaned forward more than necessary to put the hymnal away. Then I rested my hands on my lap, right over left.

John turned to me and whispered, "You said yes?"

I said okay. But I nodded anyway.

"Congratulations."

It sounded heartfelt, but I withered. I don't know why I thought he might say anything other than congratulations. He never voiced any negative thoughts about me. He was always nice, always a perfect gentleman, always keeping to himself the fact that he didn't like me. I saw it though. In his big brown eyes. They were wide open, trying to hide behind his glasses. The only thing more transparent than the glass was the disapproval that flashed as he glanced at the ring finger I was covering.

I wanted to shake him. I wanted to yell, "Just admit you don't think I'm good enough for Tyler!" I thought having it out in the open would make me feel better. I didn't say anything. I accepted his congratulations with a nod that didn't question his sincerity, and we sat quietly through church. Neither of us said much even as we walked out together afterwards.

Tyler would be waiting on the bench outside as usual. Thompsonville Christian started and ended a bit earlier. "Myrie!" he said when he saw John. "I wondered where you were this morning."

"Guess I felt like some nostalgia," he said. John grew up as a member of Sacred Heart. I'd never asked him when or why he left.

"Uh oh. You gonna take her side today?"

John just said, "We'll see," as he steered the three of us towards the parish hall for coffee and donuts.

Tyler liked to discuss the weekly sermons over coffee, comparing what I heard versus what he heard. At first, I didn't like it. It made me nervous that he was working his way towards trying to convert me. I relaxed as the weeks went on, realizing that he was simply very curious. He wanted to learn everything he could about all aspects of Christianity. He'd even considered becoming a minister himself, before he settled on the more practical career of insurance sales.

Tyler called the weekly discussions debates and tried to joke about the religious chasm between us, though we rarely found anything but common ground. I don't know how deliberate that was on his part. I knew *I* didn't intentionally bring up anything I might need to defend. And his idea of a joke was usually not all that funny anyway.

John's sister was still a Sacred Heart parishioner. He moved away from me and Tyler as we entered the hall to greet her and her family. He usually sat with her first, enjoying a donut with his two young nieces before he returned to chat with me and Tyler. We had a pretty nice routine. Though the ring on my finger changed it in some undefinable way. I did feel different that morning.

I held my coffee between my hands and watched the overhead lights shimmer in the reflection while Tyler opened his bible and took out a sheet of notes. I relied on my memory, which sometimes frustrated him.

I watched John's nieces out of the corner of my eye while we talked. They were adorable. The younger one had stubby pigtails with big bows on either side of her head. She worked on her donut very seriously. Each bite appeared carefully considered, possibly to include the most remaining sprinkles. The older one wore a frilly dress and as soon as she finished eating, she jumped out of her chair to show John some simple ballet moves.

He smiled appreciatively at her. Then he leaned over and whispered something in her ear that made her giggle. He looked my way as he stood up. My eyes dove back into my half-empty coffee cup but still noticed John's sister swooping in to hug him before he moved in our direction.

John put his white coffee cup on the other side of Tyler before he pulled out the chair. He took in Tyler's expression and furrowed his brow slightly as he said, "Pastor McAlston raking you over the coals this week?"

I sighed. "I mentioned something about the psalm today, but can't remember the number."

"It was written *somewhere* in the church, wasn't it?" Tyler sounded more irritated than usual.

I wanted to lighten his mood and said, "I didn't know there'd be a quiz."

John was the one who laughed. He sort of squinted at me and said, "You probably should've expected one by now," as he nodded pointedly at Tyler and his notes.

I laughed, too.

Tyler smiled and said, "You're right. I'm sorry." He closed his bible. "That's probably enough for today. How's Kim?"

Kim was John's sister. "They're all great," he said. "Three weeks of ballet and Olivia already thinks she knows more than her teacher." He smiled at the exuberance of the 5-year-old. It faded as he looked at me and then at Tyler. "So, uh… I guess you have some news today?"

"Oh, yeah. She said yes."

"Congratulations, man." John held out his hand.

Tyler shook it briefly before he asked John something about the next baseball game.

I said okay. Maybe that was why Tyler didn't look as excited as he should. Then again, he was a guy. They weren't the ones who got all worked up about an impending wedding. Or maybe he was holding back because he knew John thought it was a bad idea. I didn't know whether or not he knew. We never talked about John. Did Tyler sense the animosity between us? Or did they discuss it openly when I wasn't around? Maybe Tyler thought he was protecting me by not bringing it up. I knew I was protecting him. That's why I never mentioned the problem of John, for Tyler's sake.

Sacred Heart's pastor tried to stop at each table during the coffee and donut time. I saw him coming for what I knew would be a highlight of our Sunday routine. "Good morning, Monsignor Loy."

He polished off a last bite of donut. "It is pleasant, my sheep." His eyes crackled with wisdom when he looked at me, and I began to panic. What if he asked about the ring? We hadn't talked about where we'd get married. Or when. Or… anything.

I put my hands in my lap to rub my sweaty palms. Hiding the ring was a bonus. Monsignor Loy blinked, and I thought he saw something I didn't like. He didn't bring up anything serious though. "Is the music at your restaurant still…?" He appeared to struggle for the appropriate word, something critical but not derisive, and I'd heard them all already anyway.

"It is," I said simply.

"And you're getting along with that?"

"Yes." I was getting along with it just fine because I knew *why* the manager had started the novelty pirate music. "Most of the time, I don't even hear it anymore."

I heard John mumble, "That's because your ears are bleeding."

I didn't acknowledge his comment and Monsignor Loy only nodded at me before he turned to my companions. "How are you today," he mashed his lips together for a moment before he said, "gentlemen."

The pause got me every time. I put my hand over my mouth to keep from laughing out loud.

"Good, thanks," John said. He was trying not to laugh and trying not to look at me, likely because that would make him more likely to laugh.

Tyler stayed neutral with no struggle. "Excellent coffee as usual. Thanks."

"Enjoy it and the day then." Monsignor Loy moved from our table, and I swear he was trying not to roll his eyes as he walked away.

"I don't believe you," Tyler said, shaking his head at me.

The fact that he didn't see the humor somehow made it funnier to me. I made an effort to wipe the mirth from my face anyway.

He and John had started joining me for coffee and donuts after we'd been dating a few months. They hoped that between John's sister and me they had enough connection even though they weren't members of the church. They were generous with their contributions to the coffee and donut fund. They still felt guilty sneaking in and asked Monsignor Loy after a few Sundays if their intrusion was bothering anyone. The priest assured them they were welcome, but that he wasn't sure how to address those outside his flock. He called the rest of us his sheep whenever he couldn't remember a name, which was most of the time.

I knew he was only joking about not knowing what to call them, and I teased that he could call them his goats. He'd laughed at my silly suggestion and there was a pause each week as he clearly remembered it but never said it. I was still trying not to laugh something like six months later. If I managed to contain myself, John would say something as soon as Monsignor Loy left. Something like, "Glad you finally realized we're not goats," and that would pull me right back in.

Tyler, correctly, thought the whole thing was juvenile. He was telling John how confident he was that they would beat the Indians that afternoon. We'd been dating long enough that I no longer tried to make myself a Tigers fan. I just enjoyed games when I could and accepted his craziness where baseball was concerned. Though it did have a long season.

As the parish hall began to clear out, John's sister appeared at our table. "Good morning," she said. "I hear congratulations are in order over here."

I thanked her and so did Tyler.

Then she held out her hand to me. "Let me see the ring!"

I put my hand in hers. It was amazingly warm for a room with so much air conditioning.

"Aww." Kim grinned. "Have you talked dates?"

"No." I shook my head at the same time. Tyler and I had a lot to talk about.

"Oh, come here." Kim pulled me out of the chair for a hug. Her pregnant belly felt round and hard against me. "Mrs. Heidi McAlston," she said excitedly.

My stomach knotted in protest. That was going to take some getting used to. I'd been Heidi Ray for twenty-six years. "When are you due again?" I asked as she let me go.

She patted her belly. "One more month. It's a boy this time and no, we are not naming him John." She smiled at her brother, and he sighed as though he'd gotten his hopes up. He was a bad actor.

"Tyler's a good name," Tyler said.

"Sorry, but we've already picked something." Kim's younger daughter had followed her over. She picked up the toddler, then waved as she walked away.

"I guess we should pack up, too," I said.

The guys nodded and picked up their cups and napkins. Tyler took mine to the trash for me. John said, "See you later," to both of us and jogged through the parking lot. He lived in a building right next to Sacred Heart and liked to point out that coffee and donuts was on his way home.

Tyler and I walked slowly to the end of the sidewalk. He'd need to walk next door to claim his car. He held my hand as we said goodbye. "You sure you don't want to watch the game today?"

"I'm behind on laundry, and you know I need to babysit the machine."

"You could buy a new one. They sell those at a lot of stores, you know." He smiled at his own joke.

"I know. But it's only seven years old. I'm sure it has more life."

"All right. I'll see you tomorrow then." At six foot two, Tyler was exactly a foot taller than me, and I didn't wear heels that often. He had to bend down to give me a quick kiss as we parted. He walked next door to his shiny red convertible, and I returned to the parking lot to my twelve-year-old Honda.

2

I didn't need to be at work until 11 o'clock on Monday, but my alarm sounded at 6:45 as usual. I sat up so I wouldn't fall asleep again and glared at my alarm clock. Its harsh tone flashed me back to the too early mornings of high school. Tyler would call soon though, and it was easier on both of us if I was awake before the phone rang.

He liked to talk to me at the start of each day. The problem was that he liked to start his days earlier than I did mine. When he first began waking me up with phone calls, I suggested he could send good morning texts that I could respond to, you know, after the sun came up. And after I had some coffee. He said he liked to hear my voice.

That was so sweet I willingly got up earlier to hear his voice, too. I did talk him into calling a bit later though. His 7 AM calls were a compromise. By that time, he'd already gone for a run, had a shower, and eaten breakfast. I asked myself what my mornings would look like if I had a husband who got out of bed at a ridiculously early time. The answer was... a lot different. My twin bed wasn't big enough to share with anyone. I didn't want to think about change right then. Mornings, beds, husbands... change... my head was swimming in thoughts I hadn't intentionally put there.

Think about today only, I commanded myself. I shuffled into the kitchen to try to accomplish something while I waited for my phone to ring. I planned to make chili for dinner so I set my crockpot on the counter and began hunting through the cupboard for the right cans.

My can opener used to belong to my parents. The plastic covering on the handle was chipped in places so it dug into my palm if I held it wrong. The blade had gotten dull. It required strong pressure to puncture the lid and something had recently happened to the gear so that it only worked when I turned it backwards.

Tyler called as I was opening the second can. "Hello," I said, wincing as I squeezed hard to get the can started.

"Morning, baby." He sounded wide awake. "You're off at seven tonight, right?"

"Uh, yeah." That sounded like a long time away at the moment. Why was I starting a dinner we wouldn't need until then? Oh, right. Because if I'd done nothing, I'd have fallen asleep.

"John said it might be his turn to cook. Should we take him up on the offer?"

I grunted at the stupid can opener even though I was the one who forgot to turn it the other way. "No… I mean, I'm working on dinner as we speak." My voice probably betrayed how hard I was working on it.

"Something that involves cans, I'm guessing." I knew he was rolling his eyes at me. I couldn't see it, but it was in his voice.

I sighed as I finished the can and then clamped the opener onto the next one. "Chili," I said.

"Yum." Tyler sounded pleased. Then he said, "Don't hurt yourself with that can opener."

"I won't."

"It really might be time to get a new one."

I let go of the thing to give my hand a rest. "It's a perfectly good can opener," I said. "It's just too early in the morning to deal with it."

"All right. I'll let you get to your day. I love you."

"Love you, too," I said as I hung up. I mixed up the chili, reset my alarm for 9 AM, and crawled back into bed.

~~~~

The restaurant where I worked was at the end of a strip mall. I parked in the back and walked around to a side door I knew would be unlocked even though we were a few minutes from opening. Maggie, my favorite coworker, was tying on an apron as I came in. She had red hair pulled up in a curly ponytail and a smile that, as always, showed every last one of her teeth.

"Heidi!" she exclaimed. "How was your weekend?"

"Not bad," I said. "Did some overdue cleaning and now my apartment looks good."

"Awesome." The smile continued to light her face. Maggie was nineteen and for some reason I couldn't fathom seemed to think everything I did was awesome. It stoked my ego more than when I felt my younger siblings looking up to me. I guess I was old enough to admit I missed those siblings. Or at least most of them most of the time.

"Did you do anything fun yesterday?" I asked her.

"No." Maggie shook her head sadly. "This job is the most exciting thing in my life since school got out."

"I'll remember you said that when you start complaining about your classes in the fall."

Maggie grinned at me again. "Don't worry. This job will be better by then."

I only smiled back because Griffin came through the door behind me and we couldn't say anything else at that moment about why she expected the job to be better.

"Glad to see my fan club is already assembled," he said. Unlike Maggie, Griffin's smile didn't improve his features. It was phony, and it gave him an unpleasantly smug appearance.

"Hi, Griffin." Maggie forced out a polite greeting and then scurried into the kitchen.

"Heidi," he said, "I think we've missed each other for several days now. How have you gotten along without me?"

"Fine, thank you."

"With the help of some passionate fantasies, I imagine." Griffin's spikey hair was dyed a bluish white. His dark eyebrows revealed his natural color, and he wiggled them suggestively at me. "Care to share any of those fantasies?"

I knew that he knew that the only fantasy I had about him involved the door hitting him on his way out of the building for the last time. That meant there was no reason for me to say it out loud. I was relieved of the temptation by the speakers kicking on, the sign that the manager was about to unlock the front door.

Griffin looked up at the nearest speaker and swore while he made a rude gesture at it. No longer the focus of his stimulating conversation, I slipped into the kitchen after Maggie.

My first customer of the day was a woman with two small children. I'd seen them regularly and remembered that the older kid liked his lemonade without ice. The mom forgot to mention that, and she seemed truly grateful when I asked if that was still his preference. I loved my job when the people I served seemed to appreciate me.

I saw a lot of regulars as noon came and went. There were a few office buildings nearby whose employees came to us during lunch hours. A familiar group of seven sat at a big table in their business suits. They called me by name like we were all friends.

"Let me guess," I said, "one Coke, three Diet Cokes, two waters and one wildcard."

Six of them nodded that they were sticking with their standard drinks, and the last guy looked amused at the way I described his unpredictability. He made a point of being different and sometimes asked me to mix sodas. "Um… I think… I'll just have water today."

"Water?" I shook my head at him in mock disappointment. "You're letting me down."

"Oh, we can't have that," he said, causing several of his coworkers to laugh and nudge each other. "Can you bring me about two-thirds Coke with a splash of Sprite and a splash of Dr. Pepper?"

"Sure." I made a note as I asked, "And what are we calling this drink?"

"How about," he grinned, "Heidi's Approval?"

"What a coincidence," I said, "I approve of it. Do you all want to order the food now, too?"

I caught a few uncertain expressions as they looked at each other.

"Looks like we need a minute. I'll be right back with the drinks."

Griffin came up behind me later while I was putting their order into the computer. He'd evidently been on a break because he smelled strongly of cigarette smoke. "You know we can go out as soon as you admit you're interested."

"You know I'm seeing someone." Griffin didn't need to know I was engaged, though that was the moment I realized I'd forgotten to put on the ring that morning. I'd have been annoyed with myself if I'd been naïve enough to think the ring would make Griffin stop asking me out.

"Hey, I won't tell him," Griffin said. "It'll be our little secret."

I didn't say no. He knew I was thinking no. I tried to focus on what I was doing. Griffin found me at the computer a lot. I was fairly certain it was deliberate. I couldn't walk away until I was done, and it took longer when I was distracted. The large order at the moment was just his luck. Or mine, depending on whether it was good luck or bad.

"Why do you play hard to get when I see you checking me out all the time?"

I used to argue with Griffin's ridiculous assertions. But I was determined not to let him bother me and calling him out on jerky statements made my goal harder while it seemed to encourage him. Now I just tried to say as little as possible to him. I started saying the foods out loud to help me concentrate and to show Griffin that I was concentrating on something other than him.

"I've never been good at delayed gratification, but I think you'll be worth the wait."

I finished and moved away without looking at him. The glare I wanted to send would only be seen as a challenge.

He muttered, "Definitely worth it," from behind me. I could almost feel his eyes on my body, but I shrugged off any awareness of the work pest as I greeted my next customer.

James came in for lunch a couple of times a week. He had a patchy blond beard, eyes that never stayed still, and he projected a sweet personality. He'd seemed shocked when I first suggested he could use my name but had warmed up to the idea enough that he almost seemed to intentionally work it into the conversation as much as possible.

"Good afternoon, James."

"Hi, Heidi. Heidi, Mondays aren't so bad, right? Do you like working on a Monday, Heidi?"

"I like working in general. Waiting on nice people helps."

James turned a few shades of red as his eyes darted to my face and back to his menu and then to the empty chair opposite him. "Heidi... Heidi, you're a girl."

"How very astute of you."

"I mean, um..." He glanced around and rubbed a hand over his chin. "I need a girl's opinion."

"Sure."

"Is this place... would it be okay for a... a date?" James looked everywhere except at me.

"Yes." The Sleepy Crab wasn't fancy, but I thought it had romance potential. Though perhaps I was biased because I'd met Tyler at work. Either way, James looked like he needed more than a one-word assurance. "I suppose some people might not think it's ideal for a really special occasion, but for something casual... it's low pressure and there's enough variety that almost anyone can find something she likes on the menu."

James began to nod. "Okay. I thought... Well, thanks, Heidi. Heidi, your opinion settles it for me."

"Great. You want your usual Dr. Pepper and fish sandwich?"

He nodded faster. "Why mess with a good thing?"

I told him I'd be back soon and brought his drink before I delivered food to that group with Mr. Wildcard. I knew they worked at a nearby law office, though I didn't know any of their titles. When I brought their food, Mr. Wildcard asked for a refill of Heidi's Approval. His glass was only half empty. I suspected he only wanted to say the name again. I rewarded him with a sincere smile, and promised to bring more pop. They were a delightful group.

One of the other guys was singing along with the music. He embellished the slow love song about the sea with a serious expression and a hand spread against his chest. "My heart is full of salt. I can't leave it behind. My heart, it beats a salty tune. The sea, it calls to me. It calls me home." He held out the last wavering note as his companions laughed.

One of the only two women at the table widened her eyes at me. "How long is this pirate music going to last anyway?"

I shrugged. I didn't know. None of us knew if it would work to make Griffin quit faster. We only hoped. "Picking the music is not in my job description," I said, setting a sandwich in front of her.

"I like a little avast and ahoy in my music, Mateys," said a smiley guy, who was obviously joking.

People laughed. Someone said, "It's fun in small doses, but Heidi must be desperate for earplugs by the time she goes home."

"I'm used to it," I assured him. The music didn't bother me. I was telling the truth when I repeatedly told customers that it didn't bother me. I had decided not to let it. And even if the manager's plan didn't work, the people who pitied me and left bigger tips because of it seemed to greatly outnumber any complaints about the music.

3

I stopped at my apartment after work only long enough to change my shirt and pick up a crockpot of chili. My uniform for The Sleepy Crab was any black bottom and white top. I changed at least my shirt before I did anything else, even just hanging out at Tyler's place, because my clothes smelled like the restaurant after a shift. It wasn't a bad smell. Sometimes I smelled more like bacon than anything else, and I knew few people who would call that a problem. But I liked a line between work and home. I chose to draw that line at the smell.

John was already at Tyler's apartment when I arrived because the game had already started. He watched most Tigers games at Tyler's because of the bigger TV. And when I say Tyler had a bigger TV, I mean he had a TV that pretty much took up an entire wall. I think he called it a seventy-two-inch screen. I called it a monstrosity. He bought it new for the current baseball season to replace the sixty-something-inch monstrosity that was now in his bedroom.

The bedroom model replaced a smaller TV that was now in my apartment. Even that one was larger than I needed, but Tyler was going to throw it away and I couldn't watch anyone throw away a perfectly good TV. Hand-me-downs were my life anyway. There were seven kids in my family. As the second-oldest, my stuff was generally in pretty good shape. My youngest sibling, who was now eleven, could occasionally be spotted in VBS T-shirts dated with years before he was born.

My older sister, Sharon, was the only one in my immediate family who still lived in Thompsonville. She had a husband, two kids, a full-time job and not a lot in common with me anymore. We were friendly but not really friends.

Tyler and John were both Thompsonville natives, too. Tyler's dad and John's mom were from Detroit though and had trained their sons well. That's why they didn't root for a closer team. I stood outside the door holding a hot and kind of heavy pot, hoping I'd arrived during a commercial break. I tried to knock on the door with my elbow.

The TV had ridiculous speakers to go with it. I knocked again by kicking.

John opened the door and relieved me of my burden before I even crossed the threshold. "Let me get that," he said. "It smells good."

"Thanks."

He took dinner to the kitchen while I came in to greet Tyler, who looked up after a strike to say hello. At the next break in the game, we all dished ourselves some of the chili I made. John added extra chili powder. Tyler noticed something else lacking.

"You're not wearing your ring," he said.

"Oh, I forgot to put it on this morning." And apparently I forgot again when I went home to change my shirt.

"You forgot?"

I wasn't sure if it was concern or disbelief that lined Tyler's face. Whatever it was laced my dinner with guilt and made it difficult to swallow. "I just... you know I don't wear a lot of jewelry. I'm sure I won't forget again."

He nodded. He didn't look fully appeased, just distracted by the baseball game. Or maybe I was still feeling my own guilt. An engagement ring wasn't just any jewelry.

John was watching me, too. His eyes scrutinized me as though he was hoping to read a change of heart – maybe a backing out and leaving for good – into a simple memory lapse. Something that hurt worse than guilt scraped at my insides. "I worked with Griffin today," I said, desperate enough to change the subject that I picked my least favorite.

"Sorry to hear that," Tyler said. He was looking at the TV, but still listening to me.

John was equally divided. "How much longer 'til the music drives him out?"

"I wish I knew."

The Sleepy Crab was owned by a rich couple I knew only vaguely. I'd served them lunch or dinner a few times in the eight years I'd worked there. They owned several restaurants and I didn't know what else. They typically trusted the manager to keep things running smoothly without interference. Her name was Michelle Orly. I thought Michelle was a great boss. The owners, Mr. and Mrs. Dewitt, had made an exception to their hands-off policy in April when they'd contacted Michelle about a job for their grandson. Griffin.

He quickly proved himself not just onerous, but lazy, too. Michelle assigned him fewer tables than anyone else, and he still didn't keep up. He was twenty years old. He'd dropped out of college after one semester and had five jobs since then. Michelle figured she only had to wait for him to get bored.

But then she'd pulled out the pirate music on Memorial Day for a start of summer event. She didn't think pirates had much to do with summer, but it was creative. Customers thought it was a fun change. Griffin spent the entire day moaning about the ear torture. Michelle found inspiration for hastening his boredom.

"I might not see much of him this week anyway," I continued. "I only have twenty-eight hours."

Tyler pumped his fist as one of the Reds struck out. "That'll be nice. You might have time to read a few books."

"I stopped at the library on my way to work today, as a matter of fact." I tried to sound cheerful. Tyler didn't understand that a short schedule meant lost wages to me, not a vacation. He'd never known what it felt like to worry about money, and it was a subject I was too embarrassed to broach.

"Do you have any lunch shifts this week?" John asked.

"Not until Friday."

John pretended to look disappointed. Sometimes he and Tyler met at The Sleepy Crab on their lunch hours. That was how we met.

"Well," I said, "I'm feeling adventurous. I think I'll spend my day off on Wednesday trying to fix my washing machine."

"Uh…" Tyler's eyes stayed locked to the screen, but I felt his attention turning my way. "You mean you called someone?"

"No. I'm hoping I can find a YouTube video that shows exactly what I need to do."

John's hand came up to cover his mouth but not before I saw the smile he tried to hide. I realized I'd brought up money, or me trying to save some, without thinking first.

Tyler said, "Are you sure that's a good idea?"

I ignored John and tried to pretend this had everything to do with that sense of adventure I'd mentioned and not so much about the cost of a repairman. "The problem should be easy to describe to a search engine, and I won't just trust the first source I find. Plus, I think I know my limits. I won't take apart anything I can't get back together."

"Still..." Tyler put down his spoon and reached over to squeeze my knee. "It would be so much easier to pay someone. You've never fixed a washing machine before, right?"

"No. But I might be using one for the rest of my life – barring some really cool new invention – so it won't hurt to learn something. I'd rather spend the day messing with it to figure out I need help than watch a repairman only to find out it was something I could have done myself."

"You could always watch the repairman to learn how to do it next time."

"Maybe," I said. "But it's my machine so I get first crack at it."

"I think she wins," John said.

"Yeah, I give up," Tyler agreed.

Neither of them looked at anyone except the man at bat during the brief exchange. Then John glanced at me, and I saw amusement in his eyes. He thought my fear of being broke was funny. I felt completely dismissed by him.

"When are you planning this washing machine adventure?" John asked. He had turned to me fully and schooled his features into casual curiosity. But I knew what I saw.

"Wednesday," I repeated.

"I mean, what time?"

"I don't know." I shrugged. "Probably not too early and I'm not sure when I'll either be done or admit defeat."

"Do you want...?" John looked uncertainly at Tyler and then back at me. There was no commercial. "I could stop by during my lunch in case you need…" He trailed off as though he had no better idea what I might need than I did.

I didn't know how heavy the washing machine was or if I might need to move it. "Someone stronger?" I suggested.

"Or taller?" He was a few inches taller than Tyler so he really towered over me. He smiled at me in a way that really made me wish he'd just watch the baseball game.

I was stumped as to how to answer John's offer so I pretended to think about it while I waited to see if Tyler had anything to say about it.

"That's a good idea," Tyler said. He was talking to John. "You can make sure she doesn't hurt herself or flood her apartment."

John laughed. "I'm willing to bet she knows more about plumbing than I do. I'd just be a lackey."

"Right. Sorry." Tyler reached out to touch my knee again to indicate he was talking to me. "I meant that as a joke about your enthusiasm, not your competence."

"I know, honey," I said.

Tyler smiled at me without looking at me.

John was looking at me. He raised his eyebrows in a question. His offer of help was still on the table. He'd never been to my apartment. Maybe I didn't want him to see it. But maybe I didn't care if he approved or not. Maybe if I got him alone I could get him to admit why he didn't like me. But what if it was something more personal than economic status? What if it was something that reflected badly on me instead of him?

"Uh… okay," I said. "I'll try to do all the research before noon, then I'll be ready to assign heavy lifting. If there is any."

John and Tyler both said, "It's a plan," at the same time. Then I shut up and ate my dinner so they could watch the game in peace for a while. I wasn't a fan, but I did enjoy an occasional game. I liked watching baseball with people around more than most of the things I could be watching by myself. Sometimes my place was very lonely.

The door shut behind John about two seconds after the Tigers won. He wasn't oblivious to third wheels. He left as soon as the baseball game stopped being one. Tyler shut off the TV and we talked only a few minutes before I gathered my things to go. Being an early riser meant he wasn't one to stay up late.

He took the crockpot from me. "Let me carry this to your car."

"I can do it," I said. "You know it's not far."

"I do know." He tucked it under one arm. "And I know that you spoil me by cooking for me and sitting with me while I ignore you for baseball. You can at least let me walk you out." He opened his door with his free hand and gestured me through it. He held my hand as we walked down the stairs and into the small parking lot. There were only six units in his building.

"So if you're off Wednesday, maybe you can come over as soon as I get home from work and we can take a walk or something before the game. Or maybe cook together." We had arrived at my car. He took the crockpot around and placed it on the floor of the passenger seat.

"That sounds nice," I said, waiting for him to return to me.

"Good." His forehead creased. "Of course that means I'd have to buy ingredients for something between now and then." Tyler mostly lived on microwavable dinners when I wasn't around.

"It doesn't have to be anything complicated." I smiled, though trying to figure out a recipe together actually sounded like fun to me.

"I won't let you down." He bent to kiss me goodbye. Tyler had short, very dark brown hair and a matching beard that tickled my face. He'd had it as long as I'd known him. Sometimes I wondered what it would be like to kiss him without the beard.

Completely unbidden, an image of a clean-shaven man jumped into my head. It wasn't Tyler. I pushed hard against the image and the sick feeling that came with it.

4

I wore the ring to work on Tuesday. Maggie was the first to notice. She squealed that it was awesome and that I was so lucky.

Tyler was great. I *was* lucky. I spent the rest of the day thinking about being lucky and not about how I had taken the ring off three times before I decided to wear it.

I was already awake when my alarm went off the next morning. I was staring at the poster on my wall, switching the faces and goblet with my eyes and regretting that I agreed to let John come over. But if Tyler and I were going to get married...

Of course we were getting married. I said okay. *Since* Tyler and I were getting married, I thought I should try to convince John to make peace with me. But bringing up the tension when he was doing a good job pretending he was fine with everything was likely an invitation to open hostility. The humiliating history would probably come up if I tried to talk to John anyway. And he was Tyler's friend. He was the one who should talk to John. I decided to continue to act as though I didn't notice, even if that was more difficult without Tyler around.

I was cooking eggs when Tyler called.

"Morning, Heidi."

"Hi, Tyler. How was your run? Too wet?"

"Yeah. I used the treadmill today. You sound chipper."

My breakfast was beginning to smell good. "I've been up longer than usual. This is what I sound like awake."

"I like it." I could hear a smile. "Definitely a good start to my day."

"Happy to help."

"What did your coworkers say about our news?"

"Is that you asking if I remembered the ring yesterday?" I tried to sound teasing.

"Just a question," he said.

"They all said congrats. Maggie shrieked so loud customers may have thought she saw a mouse in the kitchen."

Tyler chuckled softly. It felt good to make him happy. "Sounds fun," he said. "Good luck on that little project of yours today."

"Thanks. Have fun at work."

"Always. Love you."

"Me, too."

I scooped the eggs onto a plate and set my laptop on the kitchen table to begin some research. Some of the people who post videos of repair work are nuts. And some of them need to learn about editing. One guy said he needed to run out to his garage for a tool and forgot to turn off the camera while he was gone. I clicked around forever trying to figure out where he started talking again only to realize he was fixing a problem I didn't have.

I had a pretty good plan of attack by the time John showed up. For the washing machine. I had no idea how to deal with John one on one. What if he stopped pretending I wasn't a problem? What if his real reason for coming over was to try to talk me out of marrying Tyler? While I had kept my head clear of anything awkward most of the morning, the floodgates opened the moment I heard John knock on my door. I cringed against everything I didn't want to remember.

Tyler and I had been dating nearly a year, but it had been closer to a year and a half since we first met. I met John at the same time. They became friends through a church group when they both walked in wearing Tigers fan gear. They watched games together and met for occasional lunches out. Then they discovered The Sleepy Crab. Tyler claims they were there at least twice before they landed at one of my tables. They flirted with me. Both of them. And there was nothing strange in me returning the attention. I worked for tips, and we all knew that.

Once they were established as regulars, the tone began to shift and we talked more as friends. They asked where I was from and how I felt about baseball. Eventually, they asked if I was seeing anyone and if I ever gave my number to customers. I began to hope there was genuine interest because there was on my side. I stayed hard to get for a while out of caution, but they had mentioned families and jobs and faith. They seemed like very nice guys. One day I felt a little bold and talked myself into scribbling my number on John's receipt.

I was wrong about his flirting having any meaning. He pushed me off on Tyler, who called me the next day.

I admit I was disappointed at first. But Tyler and I talked for quite a while. He called me several more times, and I found that I liked him. We were officially dating before John crept back into the picture. He was part of Tyler's life and now so was I. I guess he believed that if Tyler had any real interest in me it would fade quickly because he didn't seem to mind me in the beginning.

They were back at The Sleepy Crab the first time I noticed something amiss. Despite my best efforts at remaining professional, I slipped and called Tyler honey as I put his plate down. John didn't exactly wince, but I read the briefest moment of annoyance on his face. In the last few months, that expression had become a sore I couldn't stop picking at. I watched for those tiny flickers that meant I said or did something that bothered John. I tortured myself in the search for more proof that he disliked me or my relationship with Tyler.

John's ability to hold his tongue drove me ten times more insane than anything else. If he would say what the problem was, maybe I could defend myself. Or Tyler could defend me. But as long as John said nothing, as long as he did nothing but treat me with respect, I had nothing to accuse him of. And no way to find out if he knew I was aware of those negative thoughts floating my way. The disapproval and uncertainty swirled into a thick fog of tension between us that I had to pretend didn't exist. Or that I didn't notice it.

And yet John had volunteered to come to my apartment alone. I was half afraid of getting what I wanted. What if he was finally claiming an opportunity to tell me off?

I saw no immediate hint of that. He smiled warmly as I opened the door. "Hi, Heidi. How's the patient?"

"Uh… you mean the washing machine?" I stepped back to let him in and tried not to think about how tiny and plain my place must look to him.

"Yeah," he said. "All morning I expected to get a message that said you jumped right in and finished without needing help."

"I waited for you." Even my voice seemed smaller than usual.

"Because you thought you'd need help or…" He turned to close the door behind himself and appeared to be creating a reason not to finish the sentence.

It didn't matter what he might have said because I was only paying attention to how much space the sofa suddenly seemed to be taking up in my living room. I was standing between it and John and I felt… odd. Like the sofa might jump onto my back at any moment and push me into him. It was imperative that my washing machine be fixed as soon as possible so John could leave. "Shall we get started?" I asked.

"Lead the way," he said.

I went around the corner through my always dark – because there was only one window – kitchen and opened the door to the laundry room. The word room was applied loosely here. There was a washer facing me on my left and a dryer on my right with barely enough space to stand between them if the dryer was open. It was closed at the moment, but the space had never felt so tight.

John stood in the doorway, nearly filling it with his height. Something was different about him. He was a programmer where the dress code was relaxed, and he typically showed up at Tyler's in his work clothes. I was sure I'd seen those same jeans and blue Tigers shirt many times. That wasn't it. I didn't know what made me turn and press my back against the opposite wall as though I was afraid of him. Whatever I was feeling, it wasn't fear.

"So, uh…" John cleared his throat. "You said something about the water not shutting off?"

"Right." I banged my hand on top of the washer lid. The noise rang through the air and drove some of the discomfort from the tiny room. "Something is wrong with the thingy that

~ 25 ~

senses when it's full so it usually doesn't stop filling until I either turn the level switch a few times or if I stop it and spin the dial back around sometimes that works. But I'm afraid it's getting worse, and it might be getting to the point I won't be able to stop it without shutting off the supply valve and… well, I can barely reach those."

John nodded at me. "And what are we going to do about this problem?" He looked at me as though he thought I might have become some sort of washing machine expert in a morning of internet searches. That surprised me. My lack of a college education was probably one of the reasons he thought Tyler could do better, or so I guessed. I worried he didn't think I was capable of higher learning.

I had intended to go to college. My plan was to stay with my parents for a year or two while I saved up for it. Then my dad's job transferred him across the country two months after I finished high school. I decided to get a place of my own rather than move with the family and hunt for a new job of my own. Becoming independent could improve the financial aid package as well. Saving was more difficult once I was paying rent though. Plus, I found I enjoyed The Sleepy Crab more and more the longer I was there. It didn't seem practical to start paying for college classes until there was something else I wanted to study. At the moment, I wondered if I should have considered appliance repair.

"Well, from what I saw this morning," I said, "it might be one of two possible problems. Either the pressure switch needs to be replaced or the hose that connects it. The latter is more likely."

"That wears out more often?"

"I don't know."

"Then why do you say it's more likely?"

"Because if that's clogged, we should be able to clear it out rather than replace it."

John's laugh filled the tiny room. "So when you said it was more likely, you meant because that's what you're hoping for."

"Yes." I tried to lift my chin defiantly, but I was already looking up at him so I'm not sure it made a difference. "If I need to get a part, we're not going to accomplish anything today."

"I…" Concern flashed in his eyes before he blinked it away. I got the impression that I'd been wrong to think he was laughing *at* me. He leaned on the side of the doorframe closer to the washer and nodded at it. "Do you want to give me a job, or do I stay out of your way for now?"

If I hadn't gotten distracted with unrelated videos after I finished my research, I'd have tried to gather the necessary tools. But I'd let myself follow the clickbait. "First, I need to find something to, um…" I patted the front of the washing machine and tried to look behind him.

John realized that he was in my way and backed into the kitchen. I had the most bizarre impulse to put my hand on his stomach to push him farther away as I walked past. I retrieved a small toolbox from the floor of my bedroom closet. John was in the laundry room when I returned, and there was no way I was getting into that miniscule space with a man who… with someone that… with him.

I pointed from the doorway, or slightly behind the doorway, as I gave him instructions. "There should be two little, um, catches under this crack. All the videos showed pushing the pins down with a putty knife to take off this front cover, but I don't have a putty knife. I'm hoping this will work." I passed John a flat screwdriver.

He smiled. "Good thing my dad isn't here. He's kind of particular about tools being used only for their proper purposes." John knelt to make the crack eye level as he talked. "I think he collects tools like a hobby just so he can say, 'I have one of those,' if the need ever…I don't think this is going to work." He held the screwdriver out to me handle first. "The tip is too… not flat enough."

"Okay." I took the screwdriver and pulled a butter knife from a kitchen drawer. "Try this."

He nodded. "Yes, ma'am."

Though his tone was playful, it wasn't condescending. Where was the disapproval I was used to? It was as though John and I were actually getting along without him acting. Was it possible he was trying to bury the invisible hatchet now that my relationship with Tyler was about to become permanent?

I heard a pair of clicks as John released the front panel with the knife. "Got it," he said.

"It should be set into slots on the bottom. If you tip it towards you and then pick it up, it'll come off. But be careful for sharp edges. In this one video, the guy cut himself and kept showing shots of the blood he left on the machine like he was proud of it."

John tipped the panel back and said, "Cool. Never seen inside one of these before."

I tried not to roll my eyes. I didn't think I'd ever met a guy who didn't like to take things apart.

He set the cover aside and looked at me. "Now what?"

I looked at the exposed parts of my washing machine and had to take back the eye roll I didn't give him. It was in fact very cool in there. Better in real life than in videos. My eyes found the tube I was looking for and followed it to the bottom. It was dirty where it was attached and almost certainly clogged. Wonderful. "This is the hose and it looks like it might be clogged down there." I pointed.

John followed my finger and squatted in front of it. "So I want to take this off?"

"Yeah. All the professional people used pliers but it looks... I'm afraid that might tear it. Can you just gently wiggle it with your fingers and see if you can get it to slide off?"

He grasped the hose and began working it off the plastic nub. "You don't think those professionals knew what they were doing with pliers?"

"No, it's... well, they were replacing the hose, not trying to unclog it. I don't have a new one if anything happens to that one."

"Makes sense." The hose popped off. "There it goes. How do I clean it out?"

"Good question." I squatted next to him for a better look. "It's pretty narrow, isn't it?"

He nodded. "What does your smallest screwdriver look like?"

"That might work." I jumped up to check my toolbox. When I returned with the screwdriver, I took the hose from John and he flinched. There was an almost imperceptible jerk when my fingers grazed his. I guess that was the limit. We could get along as long as I didn't actually touch him.

I buried any disappointment as I dug the tiny screwdriver into the end of the hose. It fit, but seemed too short to reach all the way through the dirt. "This might just push the clog tighter or farther up."

"You know what we need?" he said thoughtfully. "A pipe cleaner."

"Oh, yeah. All those times we used those for school craft projects I never would have thought to use one to actually clean a pipe. But that would be the perfect thing. Too bad I'm fresh out of craft supplies."

"I bet they're cheap."

"Yeah, but..." My legs were getting tired of squatting so I tipped back to sit on the floor. John had already chosen to sit. "I hoped to get this done without having to go out or anything."

John bit his lip and turned away, trying to hide the fact that he thought something was funny.

"What's funny?" I asked.

"You."

"Why am I funny?"

"Just... your sudden impatience. How long have you been putting up with this thing?" He gestured to the washing machine. "I mean, trying to keep it from overflowing."

"I don't know." I shrugged. "Maybe two months."

"Two months. And now that you've decided to fix it, it needs to be fixed *now*." He stressed the word by tensing up all over.

It made me laugh, but I still said, "That's not funny."

"It is a little funny. I'll tell you what though," he grabbed the washing machine and used it to help himself off the floor, "I'll go buy the pipe cleaners right now. I bet they have some at the craft store around the corner."

"No, I can do it." I tried to get up and saw John holding his hand out to me. If he could pretend he wasn't avoiding contact, I could pretend I hadn't noticed the flinch. I accepted his help

~ 29 ~

and let go quickly. "You can just go back to work, and I'll find something."

He checked the clock on his phone. "I have plenty of time. I'll be back in like ten minutes."

"Let me at least give you some money for them."

"No." He walked to the door. "It's my idea so I want to pay for it in case it doesn't work. Be back soon."

He left before I could try to argue any longer. I opened my laptop – it was still on the kitchen table – and searched for videos of someone using a pipe cleaner to see if it might work for my problem. Instead, I ended up watching videos of pipe cleaner crafts. Someone did a time-lapse video making a very pretty Christmas tree. I paused it when John knocked again.

"Success," he said as I opened the door. "I got black since we intend to get them dirty anyway."

I nodded and let him back in.

"Was I supposed to get that many?" He saw the video I'd been watching.

I closed the computer. "Don't tease me about my time wasting." I tried to make my voice defensive and failed.

He smiled and said, "Sorry about the delay. Let's get back to work." He tore open the package of pipe cleaners and reclaimed a seat in front of my washer. He slid the fuzzy stick into the end of the hose and cleaned it out as well as possible. The end still looked yellowy. Then he slipped it back in place. We didn't talk as he put my washing machine back together for me.

I felt a weird anxiety about our task being finished and was happy when my phone gave me a distraction. It was a message from my granddad.

Our museum membership is up next month. Are you interested in a visit?

My grandparents lived nearly an hour from Thompsonville. We'd been close when I was a kid. But after the rest of the family left town, it became a little strange to visit them on my own. Not bad, just different. We drifted apart because of it. Then a while back, Granddad had contacted me somewhat out of the blue. He said they'd gotten a membership to the art museum and had been having a blast. He texted me repeatedly until I agreed to come check it out. We had so much fun. They invented a story for the inspiration behind each picture or sculpture. Grandma was so good she'd have me cracking up at one and near tears the next. At the end of the day, we all agreed to make the trip an annual thing.

We exchanged regular texts for a few weeks afterwards – me and Granddad, Grandma didn't like texts – but they tapered off and I hadn't heard much from them since Christmas. I couldn't help feeling this invitation seemed half-hearted. I must have been frowning at it because John asked if I was okay.

"Yeah," I said. "My granddad, um…" John didn't want to hear about my life. I put the phone away to deal with later. "I guess we're done here." I waved at the washing machine as I fought to keep myself from thinking how much different it would have been to fix it myself. I didn't want to enjoy the company of someone who only tolerated mine.

I thanked him when he left, and he said it'd been more interesting than a typical lunch hour. Interesting was one of those nice ambiguous words. He made it sound like a compliment when I was sure it wasn't.

5

Shortly before I left for Tyler's place, I got a text from Kathy. Kathy was my oldest younger sister. Her message said: Are you trying to steal my thunder?

I winced. She knew? Kathy had announced her engagement about a month earlier and was planning a wedding just before Christmas. How did she know about me and Tyler? I wanted to start simple so I typed a reply that said: What do you mean?

Kathy: Don't play dumb. Sharon saw Tyler at the grocery store. Says you're engaged.

Me: Not stealing anyone's thunder. Your wedding will still be first.

Kathy: How many bridesmaids? Do I make the cut?

I laughed at how quickly she changed from indignant to eager. I missed Kathy. She was two years younger than me, which made her twenty-four. I'd only seen her a few times a year since she was sixteen and I still pictured her as a teenager even though I knew she wasn't. I typed again.

Still working out details. Don't tell Mom and Dad until we make official announcement.

Kathy: Uh......... too late. Sorry.

Great. Mom was going to call me soon if she knew. I wondered if I should go ahead and call her first, maybe apologize for not being the one to tell her. I put my phone away. I was about to see Tyler and we needed to talk anyway. It was easy to convince myself that I should have the full story before I told my family. Being engaged meant planning a wedding, right? Tyler and I should have at least one discussion about that first so I'd be prepared for all the questions Mom would ask.

I arrived at Tyler's apartment before he did and was sitting on the steps when his car pulled into the lot and parked next to mine. I stood up and waved. He waved as well before he reached into his backseat and produced a couple of grocery bags.

"You're early," he observed as he got close enough to talk.

"Love this June weather. It's nice out, and I've been inside all day." I motioned to his bags. "Can I carry one of those?"

"Sure." He handed me a bag. "I thought maybe you were eager to see me."

"That, too," I said. And I was. I didn't know why I didn't say that first.

"What are you holding?"

"Oh, it's a spider." I glanced sheepishly at the creation I'd made from the extra pipe cleaners after John left my apartment.

"And why do you have a spider?"

"It's for John. To thank him for helping with my washing machine."

I was following Tyler up the stairs and he sent a confused look over his shoulder. "Myrie hates spiders."

"I know," I said.

"Then why are you giving him a spider?"

"Because it turns out that I'm not as creative as I hoped I'd be. He bought the pipe cleaners, and I thought I should give him the extras. They're black. Spider was all I could think of."

Tyler's shoulders moved up in a shrug as he unlocked his door. "Whatever. Is it fixed now?"

"Seems like it."

He nodded and led me straight to the kitchen. I peeked in the bag I was carrying. "What are we making?"

"I found a recipe for something called beef pinwheels. It looks kind of like meatloaf rolled up in pastry dough and sounds delicious. You're going to have to be the primary chef though. It looks complicated."

"Can I see the recipe?"

"Sure." Tyler fiddled with his phone and then set it on the counter in front of me. "I'll put everything away while you read it."

The recipe was not complicated. Tyler usually acted completely helpless in the kitchen. I knew he could cook though. He just didn't like to. He put the new things away while I figured out a plan for dinner.

"I saw your sister when I was at the store yesterday," Tyler said from behind me.

"Yeah?" I bit my lip about the fact that Tyler went shopping too often. And I wasn't so distracted that I couldn't say I knew he'd talked to Sharon. I wanted to see what he said about it first.

"She was surprised when I mentioned the engagement."

That sounded like a straightforward statement. I heard the question though. He wanted to know why I hadn't told her. It was probably time to talk about that. I left the recipe on the counter and turned to face Tyler. "I wanted to have more details before I told my family."

"Details?" He appeared more concerned than confused.

"You know the first thing anyone will say – it's the first thing anyone has said so far – is to ask about a date. I thought we should have at least a ballpark timeline or... something."

He nodded. "Yeah. We haven't talked about that."

"And if we're going to have... I'm assuming you want your pastor involved as well as Monsignor Loy and that might... I don't know how well their calendars line up."

"Right." Tyler stroked his beard thoughtfully. "I'll make an appointment with the pastor soon to get his take and then we can start to... work on that."

"Okay."

"Okay. So... dinner?"

"Yes, dinner." I'd much rather think about dinner than the fact that what Tyler and I just agreed to was to put off talking about a wedding date. I focused on the recipe and began asking him for supplies. We spent a lot more time cooking and eating at Tyler's place. Even though I'd mostly learned where things were kept, we still worked rather like I was the surgeon and he was the nurse. I said what we needed and he produced it and handed it to me.

He talked about his job while I squished the meat mixture with my hands. I kept them under the running water longer than necessary to clean up because it was so cold my fingers had

~ 34 ~

turned red. I spread the meat next, rolled it up into the pastry and began to slice it.

"We should throw out the end pieces since they don't have as much meat as the rest," Tyler said. "That's more than we can eat anyway."

"What?" I turned to him incredulously. "It may be more than we can eat *now*, but that doesn't mean we shouldn't save it. I'm not going to throw out perfectly good food."

Tyler opened his mouth to say something. Then he closed it. His second thought was, "You know you say that a lot."

"Say what?"

"Perfectly good. You say something is perfectly good and usually what you mean is… this is broken, but I've decided to be stubborn about getting rid of it."

"But this is really…" I pointed at the pinwheel in question. It didn't look as good as the ones in the middle, but who were we trying to impress? We could still eat it. It was… I was just going to say it. "It's a perfectly good pinwheel."

Tyler cracked a smile. "This time I'll have to agree that's edible. But what about… that twenty-year-old can opener you're still using, or the washing machine that nearly overflows or… oh," he sighed heavily, "the remote with the broken five."

"That's a… *fine* remote."

"Except that when you push the five, nothing happens."

"But all the other numbers work." We'd talked about the remote before. It came with the TV Tyler passed to me and the five somehow stopped working in the transfer. He'd offered to replace it, but I wouldn't accept it. I didn't understand how he could feel guilty when it wasn't his fault and he'd already given me a whole TV. "If you want a channel with a five, you punch in something near it and use the up and down buttons. It's not difficult."

"No. It's not difficult. But it's annoying as all get-out."

"Speaking of things people say a lot…" I tried to make my face serious. "What does *all get-out* mean?"

Tyler appeared to give the matter real thought before he smiled at me. "I have no idea. You win. I'll even be the one to eat the perfectly good pinwheel."

I turned back to finish slicing them, not feeling like I won anything. I felt like Tyler only wanted to end the conversation. "Then I better get these in the oven. Though I will concede your point about this being too much for us. Is John eating here?"

"Um… he knew we planned to eat before the game so he was going to eat before he came over, too." Tyler grabbed his phone from the counter. I was done with the recipe. "I'll let him know we'll have leftovers though."

Once the food was cooking, Tyler suggested we take a quick walk. We only went once around the block. At one point, we passed another couple on the other side of the street. They were walking three dogs. Tyler muttered something that sounded like, "Poor guy."

I asked him what he said.

He pointed across the street with a slight nod of his head. "I said, 'Poor guy.'"

"Why do you say that?"

"I'm betting he's interested in that girl and she's not in his league."

I thought they were a cute couple. "What makes you think they're not already married or something?"

"Doubt it," he said.

I heard the words of our brief exchange rattling in my head for the rest of the walk while I tried to figure out why they bothered me. He'd never said anything like that about me and the thought popped into my head that perhaps he didn't consider me much of a prize. I dismissed that as either vain or stupid. Then I tried to convince myself I should be jealous that he'd apparently thought the other woman was attractive. I could objectively say that she was pretty though, and I didn't *want* to be jealous. I was almost sure I was bothered that I wasn't bothered and that didn't even make sense. Tyler and I had a nice, secure relationship. He told me he loved me all the time. It was almost always at the end of a phone call, like a reflex. That only meant we were comfortable. Why was I questioning comfortable?

Tyler was right about the dinner being delicious. I enjoyed the meal, even though we rushed a little to finish before the game started. The first pitch had been thrown by the time John arrived. He rushed in to see if he missed anything. On the first break, I presented him with the pipe cleaner spider. It was a little smaller than my hand and looked smaller in John's. The man was all arms and legs and though I hadn't seen it, I was pretty sure he could palm a basketball.

"What's this?" he asked.

I stated the obvious. "It's a spider."

"I can tell. Why did you make a spider? I thought you were going to keep these in case you needed to clean out the hose again."

"I kept a few. I thought you should have the extras as a thanks. But I didn't think you'd have a use for them either so I made them into a decoration."

Both the guys were looking at me as though I had done something weird. Because I had.

"I was bored this afternoon. Okay?"

Tyler shrugged at John. "Sorry, Myrie. She claims to know you're not a fan of spiders."

"That's all right," John said. "I get it."

"What do you get?"

"She didn't need any help today. This is a thanks for nothing present." John's faint smile told me he was teasing, but that wasn't what stopped my protest. It was the way he very gently set the spider on the arm of his chair as though giving it a place of honor.

Tyler's living room was set up with two nice recliners directly in front of the TV and a small, tan loveseat in a corner. The guys sat in the chairs when the Tigers were playing. They'd both tried to offer me what they considered the best seats, but I really preferred to be where I could see them as well as the TV. Their synchronized reactions to both good and bad plays reminded me of watching sports with my dad, though his passion was football and not baseball.

I think it was about the third or fourth inning that Tyler was watching intently when John moved the fuzzy black spider. He slowly took it off his armrest and set it on the back of Tyler's chair, just to the right of his head.

When there was a break in the action, he turned to say something to John and didn't notice the spider. He did eventually notice that I looked tense because he wrinkled his eyes curiously at me. I'm not sure if I was looking at John or the spider, but Tyler turned that way again and jerked up when he caught sight of my pipe cleaner creation. "Myrie!" he exclaimed. "That's not funny. I almost squashed that thing."

John took it back but didn't appear terribly remorseful. Maybe he'd hoped to see it squashed. I probably wasn't pulling off my innocent expression very well because I felt like I'd been in on it. Tyler simply sighed and went back to watching the game.

It was a long one. I think it was the bottom of the tenth inning when Tyler fell asleep. That was a consequence of running at an hour when normal people were still in bed.

A little later I saw John open his mouth to say something. He glanced at Tyler. I thought perhaps he had forgotten that Tyler was sleeping. Then he crossed the room to take the seat next to me.

I picked up my phone, thinking I might "accidentally" make enough noise with it to wake Tyler. The feeling that I needed his protection was so unexpected that I hadn't processed how dumb it was until after I'd picked up the phone.

I reread the text from my granddad to cover the unnecessary movement. I hadn't responded yet so I quickly typed out: How about Monday?

Then I cautiously lifted my eyes to John as I put the phone down.

"Is something going on with your grandparents?" he asked. "I just... you look worried."

They weren't the reason I looked worried. I tried to explain anyway because I needed to say *something*. "We were supposed to make this museum trip an annual thing, but now they're asking me to go because the membership is going to expire and if they're letting it expire, they must not... I hate to think they're inviting me now out of some sort of obligation."

"You don't think they want to see their granddaughter?"

"I'm sure they do." He'd only come closer so he could keep his voice low. But he brought with him that familiar tension, that crushing feeling that I couldn't say anything that would meet with his approval. "It's just that… Well, I miss *them* so I suggested Monday."

John nodded at the way I closed the subject. He said, "The washer was working fine this afternoon?"

"Yes," I said. "Two loads without a problem."

"How long do you think before you can run it without feeling like you need to watch?"

I smiled in spite of the dense air because I'd been thinking the same thing all afternoon. "I fully expect to watch it until the load *before* it tries to overflow again."

"That'd be perfect." He was trying not to laugh out loud and there was a rumble in his voice. "It wasn't too bad the last time though, was it?"

I shook my head. "I was right there in the kitchen so I saw the water right away and shut it off and mopped everything up before there was any damage. Though it's a good thing I live on the first floor."

Those dark eyes widened as he nodded in agreement.

"My apartment is so small I should be able to catch it early if it does happen again. As long as I'm home."

John turned back to the TV when a commercial ended as I finished talking. Two thoughts competed for attention in my head.

The first was that I could still feel John sitting next to me even though he wasn't actually touching me. I wanted him to move back to the recliner so I could concentrate on obsessing over the second thought, which was that my home might not be my home much longer. I'd almost certainly move in with Tyler when we got married. His apartment made more sense because it was bigger. It was closer to The Sleepy Crab and to Sacred Heart and… well, Tyler's apartment was about the only other place I went regularly. It made sense.

My lease was up in August though. That wasn't enough time to plan a wedding. When I thought about having an excuse to push the wedding to more than a year in the future, I felt something too close to relief.

Granddad replied to my text with: Great. The museum is closed on Monday. It has great exhibits

on the walking trail though and the weather
is supposed to be good.

It sounded as though they still wanted me to come, but if the museum was closed it might not be the same. I kicked myself for not remembering the museum was closed on Mondays. Then I stopped thinking about almost everything and watched some baseball.

The game lasted thirteen innings and ended near midnight. John turned off the TV and Tyler still didn't wake up. We left him slumped in the chair and showed ourselves out.

6

I worked until close on Thursday, which was unfortunate for a lot of reasons. Griffin was one of them. While I was sure he still annoyed everyone, he seemed to be focusing his efforts on me. He kept accusing me of denying my true feelings for him, and I began to wonder how much longer I could ignore him. The Tigers got rained out that night so I missed a chance to do something different with Tyler. We could've watched a movie or played a game or anything that was not baseball. I also missed a call from my mom. It was time to have that conversation. Friday might prove eventful.

Tyler called me first thing as usual. I was pretending to choose some breakfast but really only staring absently at the contents of a cupboard. I wasn't awake enough to make decisions that did not involve a coffee flavor. "Morning, Heidi," he said. "How was work last night?"

I think I may have grunted into the phone as I tried to remember. "The usual mostly. Thursday evenings are quiet."

"Myrie and I met some guys from church for basketball. It's been too long since we've done that."

"Sounds like you had fun."

"Yeah. We're talking about doing it again Saturday. Would you mind if we had lunch instead of dinner that day? Unless you want to play?"

"Ha. Have you forgotten how tall I am? You guys would step on me."

"So lunch is okay? I tried to get the guys to do it in the morning, but Myrie likes to sleep in and he sided with the others."

When he didn't even acknowledge my joke attempt, I thought maybe Tyler was the one still asleep. "Lunch is fine," I said.

"Great. Don't forget Myrie's bringing food tonight so you're off the hook."

"Okay. I'll see you after seven."

"I love you."

"Love you, too. Bye." I hung up and went back to the bedroom to bury my face in my pillow. When I got up again an hour later, that cupboard in the kitchen was still open and I felt more ready to start my day.

My closet had a few dresses and nicer things for church, a few casual jeans and T-shirts, and a black-and-white section that was my work clothes. I chose a skirt for a change and pulled out a white top I hadn't worn for a while. It was pretty but awkward to put on. The top half of the back was scooped out and a string at each shoulder tied the sleeves together at the back of my neck to keep them from falling down. The problem was that if I tied it too tightly, the material pulled uncomfortably under my arms. And if it was too loose, the sleeves would slip off my shoulders and that wasn't comfortable either. Since I had to put my arms in the air to reach the ties, it was hard to judge and I had to retie it several times to get it just right. I think it took five times that day.

I got out the hairdryer, which started fine. But it shorted out before I was done. I knocked it into my palm like a simple reflex and got it going. Then I piled my hair into a loose bun and smiled at my reflection. I looked nice and that was a bit of a confidence booster. I would need that confidence since I had gotten ready early to call my mom before work.

She picked up right away.

"Hi, Mom. You home?" She put in a lot of volunteer hours at the church now that everyone was in school or out of the house, but if I remembered correctly, she was typically home on Fridays.

"Yes," she said. "Just stripping the beds." I could picture her stopping to sit on one as she answered my call. "I've been hoping to hear from you for a few days now."

"I hear someone let the cat out of the bag."

~ 42 ~

"You can still tell me yourself. You do have news, right?"

"Tyler asked me to marry him."

"Yea!" Now I imagined her holding up her free hand to cheer. "Congratulations, honey. When's the big day?"

"I don't know yet. That's why I didn't call sooner. We still have some things to work out."

"Heidi." Mom sounded suddenly serious. "Do you *want* to marry him?"

"What!? Of course I do, Mom."

"It's just… you don't sound very excited."

Didn't I? Maybe I still had some waking up to do because I *was* excited. "You know Kathy's the emotional one. I'm happy, Mom."

"Good. You start giving me the details as soon as you have them."

"I will." I let her talk for a while. It was nice to hear about my three siblings who still lived at home. Then I had to cut her off so I wouldn't be late for work.

I was tying on an apron when Griffin came in. He nodded approvingly at my appearance. "Wow, Heidi. You look hot today. The customers will all be jealous of me."

I didn't let him bait me. "Good morning, Griffin."

He smiled as though I'd said something scintillating. "You shouldn't undress me with your eyes while we're at work."

I walked away rather than respond. The first couple I waited on looked around the same age as my grandparents. The woman exclaimed, "Oh, my! Aren't you lovely?" before I could open my mouth.

"Thank you, ma'am, and welcome. Have you eaten here before?"

"We discovered this place only recently and just knew it'd be perfect to celebrate our 60th anniversary."

"Sixty years?" I said. "Congratulations to both of you."

"I'm the one to be congratulated," the man said as he reached a hand across the table to his wife. "Still don't know how I got this prize to stick around so long."

She smiled demurely as she also reached out, then playfully swatted his hand away. "Doesn't she look just like Julie when she was younger?"

He nodded but kept his eyes on his wife.

"Can I start you with something to drink?" I asked.

"Julie is our youngest daughter." The woman turned to me with a faraway expression. It seemed she was facing me but focused on a picture in her head. "She looked so much like you when she went away to school. She came home that first Christmas all starry-eyed over a guy. Then she suddenly became accident prone. We were afraid he was hurting her. Turns out she had a tumor causing balance problems. The man we accused of hurting her stood by through the whole ordeal."

"I'm sorry," I said. I'd had others spontaneously share personal stories and hadn't come up with a better response. "That sounds difficult."

"It was, dear. But don't worry. There's a happy ending. They've just had their first grandchild." She smiled brightly as the couple appeared to remember they were in a restaurant and placed drink orders.

I recognized three guys who came in regularly from a nearby office. One of them was named Mark, but I wasn't sure whether it was the short, blond one or the muscular one with the goatee. I was sure that the third one had never ordered anything other than the shrimp tacos.

"Afternoon, gentlemen," I greeted them. "How glad are we that it's Friday?"

"Very," the blond one said.

The beefy guy in the group smiled broadly. "Happy Friday to you, Heidi. You always ask to have us put at your table, don't you?"

"Of course." I winked at him. "Don't tell the other girls though. They'll be jealous."

He laughed good-naturedly.

"What would you like to drink?" I met the eyes of the first possible Mark.

"Diet Coke," he said.

I nodded and got drink orders from the other two.

When I went to the kitchen, one of the cooks asked me to take out an order that had been sitting for a while. One of Griffin's tables. I brought the sandwiches out to two middle-aged women. "Here you are, ladies. Sorry about the delay. Who had the turkey club?"

One of them raised a hand slightly. I set the dish in front of her.

"And a Reuben?"

The other woman wrinkled her nose.

"No? What did you order?"

"Shrimp tacos."

"That's not the same as a Reuben at all, is it?"

She smiled at me.

"Let me find out what happened. We'll get that to you as soon as possible." I took the Reuben to the kitchen and put together the shrimp tacos myself. I hadn't worked there for eight years and learned nothing. When I was caught up again, I cornered Griffin and told him to fix the check for his table.

He jerked his head towards the computer. "Come show me how again."

I followed him over, but he tried to get me to hold his hand, literally, through the steps on the touch screen. I didn't have time for his contrived incompetence. I reminded Griffin how to finish and left him.

I brought the food out to my three lunching men. "Let's see," I said. "I have some shrimp tacos here. Who ordered those today?"

All three of them laughed and one guy pointed to himself rather meekly.

"We all have our weaknesses," I said.

"What's yours?" asked the blond guy, who wore glasses with black frames and was raising his eyebrows at me behind them.

"Oh, I can't tell you that," I said, placing a plate of food in front of him. "You'd all be bringing me chocolate cheesecake and asking for favors."

More laughter all around the table. This was a fun group.

"You all let me know if you need anything else."

They nodded at me as they began to dig in.

Griffin came up behind me next time I was punching an order into the computer. "What time do you get off?" he asked.

"Seven." I didn't look up from what I was doing.

"Me, too," he said. "I'm available if you're ready to admit you want me."

"I'm not." I meant not available, but I realized too late how he might take my answer.

"I can feel your eyes on me all across this place. You'll have to give up and admit it soon."

I gathered up some of that determination not to let him bother me. Ignoring him wasn't working though. I took a deep breath, looked right at Griffin and said, "I'm sorry if that's bothering you."

His surprised laugh followed me to my next table. I'd never made him laugh before, and it gave me a strange sense of power. I felt like I could say he didn't bother me and fully mean it.

That older couple was very sweet as they were leaving. The woman told me two more times how pretty I looked and I didn't know if she repeated herself on purpose or not, but I didn't care. The man complimented the food as though I made it all by myself just for him.

Maggie came in late in the afternoon to help with dinner. "Hi, Heidi!" She greeted me with that toothy grin that made smiling back not optional. "You look awesome today."

"Thanks, Maggie."

"Was Tyler here for lunch?"

"Not today."

"He's got to come in when I'm here anyway so I can tell him congratulations." Maggie looked at my hand while she talked and bounced on her heels as her eyes danced around my ring. I was thinking that her mom would never accuse her of not sounding excited.

A large group came in for an early dinner. We pushed together two of my tables and one of Griffin's to accommodate the party of eleven. That meant he was supposed to help me. I'd probably be better off doing it myself. I brought out drinks without a problem but then the men in the group tried to make things difficult for me. Man number one asked if I could split the check into three. I said that was fine.

"All right," he said. "I'll be paying for myself, that woman in the blue shirt, and the kid in the high chair next to her."

I nodded and took his order. Man number two said that he was covering himself, the woman in the red shirt, and all four of the other kids. I figured out what everyone wanted to eat and thought the checks were clear until man number three said, "My check should include her," he pointed to the woman in the blue shirt, "and the two blond boys."

When I explained why that confused me, half the table had a discussion about whether a light teal shirt could more accurately be described as blue or green. I might have laughed at the seriousness with which the topic was addressed except that I'd already matched the couples and just needed them to tell me who was claiming the kids.

"Some days none of us want to claim them," man number three said.

Most of the adults laughed. The oldest child, a girl who looked around ten, gave a dirty look to man number two, who might have been her dad.

"Today though," I said. "Who's claiming which kids for the purpose of this meal?" I pointed to my notepad hoping that I didn't sound impatient. I really wasn't. I just wanted them to help me get it right.

Man number two reminded man number three about some movie tickets that didn't seem to have anything to do with anything. But then man number three relented to pay for only him and his wife, who may or may not have been wearing a blue shirt. I didn't write that down. I rushed to the computer to enter everything while I could still make sense of my notes.

The odor of cigarette smoke hit my nostrils to warn me of Griffin's proximity. "You're too nice," he said. "You should have told them you'd put it all together and let them sort it out."

"Thanks for your help," I said. He was telling me that he'd been standing close enough to watch me take the order, which was annoying even though I knew one more person in that conversation would not have simplified it.

"Didn't want to distract you with all the hormones that are active when I'm too close." He took a small step closer.

I was partially ignoring him, not because I was pretending to concentrate but because I was actually concentrating. "How considerate," I said.

He leaned against the wall next to the computer so that I could see him out of the corner of my eyes. "I have my moments," he said. "You ready to see some of them outside of this place?"

"No." I tapped the last button and looked up. "I prefer to torture myself."

One corner of his mouth lifted but another coworker nudged him before he could say anything.

"They're waiting on you in the kitchen, man," the other guy said.

Griffin rolled his eyes and apparently went back to work.

I didn't see him until it was time to bring out the food for our shared table. I told him I needed him and that got his attention long enough to put a tray in his hands. I was printing receipts when he came up behind me yet again. "After all the compliments you send my way, it's only fair to tell you how much I love your shirt."

"Thanks," I said. Sincerely, because that might have been the least outlandish thing he'd ever said to me.

"It makes me think I could just pull this string and watch your clothes fall off."

So much for normal compliments. I sensed his hand near my back and instinctively jerked away. The string tugged and loosened my sleeves. Fortunately, my shirt didn't actually fall off. I'd just be pushing the sleeves back onto my shoulders until I could get it retied. I was mostly annoyed because I knew how many times it would take to get it right again. "Griffin!"

I didn't say more than his name because he seemed genuinely startled by what he did. "I didn't... Just let me fix it," he said.

"I can—"

"Hold still a second." Griffin grabbed the strings and I had two credit cards I needed to return so I stood there and let him retie my shirt. He was quick, but he tied it too tight. I had only a half hour left on my shift so I could handle the chafing. I put the receipts on the tables and passed Maggie on my way to the kitchen. She was carrying a tray and singing along to the music.

I mouthed, "Yo ho ho," at her.

She tried to smile sheepishly but didn't really have anything less than a full grin. "I don't even know when I'm doing it," she said.

Griffin was already outside when I left for the day. He was having a smoke before getting into his car.

I simply waved at him.

He called, "Wear that when we go out so I can untie it on purpose."

I waved again, over my shoulder.

He was chuckling at how he'd amused himself, any remorse apparently forgotten.

I drove to Tyler's feeling more excited about baseball than usual. I was just really worn out and looking forward to an evening of good company in front of a TV. It sounded relaxing, especially since someone else was cooking.

I went straight to the bathroom after John let me in. Because I hadn't stopped at home first, I brought a clean shirt to change into. That's when I discovered Griffin had tied a knot in the strings. On the *back* of my shirt. I probably should have changed first and then worked on undoing the knot, but I didn't think of that in the moment. I only thought that I had a knot behind me and someone in the next room who could help.

I went back to the living room and found John sitting by himself in front of a muted commercial. "Where's Tyler?" I asked.

"Said he left something in his car."

"Oh. Can you help me then? There's a knot." I turned around and pointed to the back of my neck.

He didn't say anything. I glanced back and saw him getting out of the chair though. That was a yes. He shouldn't have needed more than two steps to reach me. I seemed to be waiting longer than that. I was about to turn to see if perhaps he had misunderstood my problem when I felt the string gingerly lift off my skin. The brush of fingertips caused an unexpected shiver that rippled down my back and my arms.

My eyes closed on their own, and I was overwhelmed by the sensation that John was about to kiss the back of my neck or put his arms around my shoulders or something else that might make both of us forget there was a knot. He continued to gently

~ 49 ~

tug on the fabric while goosebumps cropped up on what I was sure was every inch of my body.

Very softly he said, "There you go," and I sensed him move away.

Tyler came in holding a magazine, and I returned to the bathroom to finish changing. I felt flushed but didn't detect any color on my face so I came out quickly and tried to act naturally.

"What's for dinner?" I asked the guys.

John was staring at the screen intently even though it was a dog food commercial.

"Lasagna," Tyler said.

I thought I smelled something like that.

"It's just staying warm in the oven," John said, still not looking at me and for that I was grateful. "You can help yourself if you're hungry."

"I'll dish it up." I needed to move so I could outrun my thoughts. I focused my mind on lasagna. On getting plates. On how much Tyler might like to eat. On bringing it to him. On a second plate. Not on who it was for. Just the lasagna I was carrying.

John said, "Thanks."

I was already back in the kitchen. There was more lasagna. I was hungry, too. I sat with a plate on my lap and Tyler muted the TV to pray over our food.

Then baseball wasn't enough of a distraction. "This is good," I said.

"Thanks." John kept looking at his plate. "You don't have to sound surprised."

"I didn't." Maybe I did. Maybe guilt sounded like surprise. But I wasn't thinking about that. "Anything interesting happen at work today? Anyone?"

"Not really," Tyler said.

"I wrote code. Answered emails." John glanced at me. "The usual."

"I keep catching Maggie singing," I said. "She's funny when she realizes what she's doing."

The guys might have been listening. I didn't get much reaction though.

"Griffin's current favorite seems to be to accuse me of undressing him with my eyes."

Tyler rolled his. "I thought you were just ignoring him."

"I am. Mostly."

"He's not..." John stopped looking at the screen to study me instead. "He's just obnoxious, right? You've never felt... threatened by him?"

I shook my head and watched my fork dig into my dinner until I was sure John had turned away. "I have the whole weekend off now."

Nodding greeted my declaration. Tyler already knew that.

"Off until Tuesday actually." My mouth just needed to move. It didn't seem to matter how inane my chatter. "Church on Sunday of course." Of course. "Baseball, too." Always. I didn't need to remind anyone there of a baseball game. "And, um... we'll have lunch tomorrow." I was looking at Tyler, but I still saw it. I saw that almost undetectable squinting that said John wished I would go away. Though at the moment, he may have just wished I'd shut up. "I might go back to school."

"This weekend?" Tyler looked confused and distracted.

John put down his fork and looked away from the pitcher on the screen but not entirely at me. His face didn't seem to say, "I don't think you're capable of that," or "It's too bad you haven't done school already." It was more like, "What the heck made you bring that up out of the blue?" He likely thought I was an idiot for even trying to get him to sanction my existence.

"I meant later," I said. "I don't know. I sometimes think I should still go to college."

Tyler glanced at me for a moment and said, "Okay."

John said, "Why?" Then he shifted in the chair as though he was mentally kicking himself. "I meant... you don't need a degree for your job and you seem to really like it. Is there something else you want to do?"

"No."

"You *are* happy there?"

"Yeah. Never mind." I clamped my mouth shut and let them watch the game. I was happy at The Sleepy Crab, even when Griffin was making absurd remarks at me. He never bothered me nearly as much as the awful thing that I felt only a few minutes earlier. I knew I hadn't imagined that John might make some romantic move because there was any chance he would but because I wanted him to. That was the dreadful truth I was trying not to admit to myself.

I had more sense than to be attracted to a man who didn't even like me. I'd put a stop to those feelings a long time ago. How could I let it happen now? I was engaged. I said okay. My decision to *not* be attracted to John Myrie had never been up for reevaluation, and it certainly wasn't now.

7

I know I don't make good decisions first thing in the morning, but I'm not sure even the early hour can account for why I thought adding more guilt was going to help my guilty feelings.

I woke up thinking about John. I don't know if he appeared in a dream – which I would have had no control over – or if some other fluke snuck him into my head. I felt so guilty that I hadn't moved away when he was working on my knot the night before. I couldn't convince myself that I hadn't done anything wrong because there was nothing to move away *from*. But I felt so guilty anyway that I ignored Tyler's morning call and then felt worse for ignoring him.

He left me a brief message that said he was looking forward to seeing me soon. An irrational fury lit inside me when I heard those words. I was angry that he called when he was going to see me in a few hours and that was like being angry because he cared about me. I didn't exactly feel guilty about that. Just wrong. Feelings could be wrong.

I got myself and my inexplicable fury sorted out before Tyler came over. I thought I was as excited to see him as when we first started dating. It's possible, however, that I was only remembering what it felt like to be nervous.

Tyler arrived with a package. It wasn't a pretty paper with ribbons kind of package. It was a white plastic bag that I could see through, and it made me more nervous.

"I brought you something," he said as he reached into the bag and pulled out the still attached to a cardboard label and fresh from the store can opener. He thrust it into my hands.

I said, "Thanks."

I did not point out that he knew I already had a can opener. Or that it was a perfectly good can opener. I set the new one on my kitchen counter and we sat and talked for a bit. He was still not over the fact that not only had he fallen asleep during a Tigers game, but that neither John nor I bothered to wake him up. He told me a bit about the guys he was meeting for basketball later. I had met only one of them before. Other than John of course.

When I asked Tyler if he wanted to start on lunch and he said he did, we moved into the kitchen where he could watch me. Immediately, I faced the most manufactured dilemma I'd faced since I lived with a house full of siblings. I intended to fry up some salmon patties for lunch, which required opening a can.

That new can opener was sitting right in front of me, and I didn't want to use it. I knew it would be petty to insist on using the old one. I swallowed that impulse and took the packaging off the one Tyler brought. I could use the old one when he wasn't around. That would still be petty of course, but he wouldn't know. I emptied the can into a bowl and added a few ingredients.

While I was mixing it up, Tyler said, "You're going to keep that old one anyway, aren't you?"

"The old can opener?" I made my voice casual, as though I hadn't been thinking about anything as trivial as can openers. "Sure. It won't hurt to have a backup."

"You didn't feel the need for a backup for the one that was actually falling apart." There was an argumentative edge to his voice.

Rather than attempt to diffuse the conversation, I chose to meet his challenge. "I'd have gotten one if I thought I *needed* one."

"You think I'm wasteful. With money."

Where did that come from? I grabbed a pan from a cupboard, shutting the door a bit more forcefully than I should have, then set the pan on the stove to heat up. "I didn't say that. I just think we have a different idea of what constitutes a necessity."

"Clearly," Tyler said, "because I think you'd have an easier time opening a can if you beat it with a rock."

"That's not an exaggeration at all," I said, turning away so he wouldn't see my eyes swiping the ceiling. "Just because you don't know how to make do with what—"

"I do know."

"You've never had to—"

"Yes, I have."

"I've seen your parents' house."

"That's not the house I grew up in, you know."

"I know." I sort of knew. Tyler had mentioned at some point that they'd only lived in that house a few years, but he'd never elaborated on their old house.

"You know my dad didn't finish law school until I was fourteen. Things were much tighter before that. I know what it's like to wear thrift store clothes. I know what it's like to envy the things my friends treated carelessly and I know how to make do. But I don't want to make do when I don't have to. I have a good job that I worked for and you're not as destitute as you like to think you are. I know you could afford a fifteen dollar can opener – you probably have more money in the bank than I do – but you get some sort of perverse pleasure out of using something past its normal lifespan."

I dropped the last of the salmon into the pan and began to scrub my hands. The motion did not help me calm down. We'd argued before, but this felt different. There hadn't been speeches before. This felt like something he'd wanted to say for a while. And I was holding back a longer response. Even if I hadn't said it, I did think he was wasteful with money. "Most people consider a rainy day fund a good thing," I said. I felt as much as Tyler did that I wasn't trying to appease anyone with those words.

"You don't save money," he said. "You hoard it. You make me feel guilty any time I want to enjoy something I've earned. I think you even resent what I spent on that ring." He gestured to the shiny circle on the counter. I'd taken it off while I was cooking and was about to put it back on.

It was so small and I had never bought myself any jewelry. I really didn't know and hadn't thought about how much it might have cost. Its purpose was more significant than money and as I slipped it back onto my finger, what Tyler had spent on it was the last thing I wanted to know. "I'm sorry," I said. "Sorry if I've ever made you feel guilty. You obviously have a right to do whatever you want with your own money."

He nodded slowly while we both took a few relaxing breaths. "I'm sorry, too," he said. He pulled me in for a hug. I felt his chin rest lightly on top of my head. "What are we having with the fish?"

I happily let him change the subject, and we had a calm lunch. After he left, I considered throwing away my old hand-me-down can opener. I shoved the new one to the back of the drawer instead. It might be better, but now it had a bad memory associated with it.

~~~~

"We should talk."

That was the first thing Tyler said to me Sunday morning. Mostly. He said, "Good morning," when he and John met me outside Sacred Heart and he said a few other pleasantries on the way to the parish hall. But when John met up with his sister's family and Tyler and I sat down with cups of coffee, he didn't open his bible. He didn't extract the sheet of notes I saw sticking out of it. He said, "We should talk."

His expression was grave so I tried to appear open to whatever he needed to say.

"I'm sorry about yesterday."

"Me, too," I said. "I—"

"Wait." He put his hand up. "It was my fault. I wanted to say this yesterday, but I got nervous and picked a fight instead." He paused and watched his finger trace the edge of his cup. "The thing is... I think I made a mistake."

His eyes flickered to my left hand, and I knew what he was talking about.

"Please understand," he continued in a rush, "I'm not trying to break up with you. I still... I just think maybe I jumped the gun with an engagement."

My hands moved from my paper cup, and I began to twist the ring around my finger. "Can I ask... why did you ask me if you weren't sure?"

"Blame Myrie."

"John told you to propose?" That didn't make any sense. Tyler must have missed some sarcasm.

"Not exactly." Tyler was squirming. I could see how worried he was about my reaction. "Not at all. Don't blame him really. We were talking about marriage in general, and I don't know how it even came up. But he said something like I must have spent enough time with you to at least have an idea if we were headed that way. I thought... I knew I didn't want to end it so..." He shrugged rather helplessly.

I pulled the ring halfway off my finger. "I, um... I think I only said yes because I didn't want to break up either. I'm really... not sure." I held the ring out to him.

"So this is good?" he said as he took it. "We're on the same page. This is not us breaking up. We're just agreeing to take a little more time before..." He nodded at the hand closed around an engagement ring. There was a tiny circle in that hand that wanted to be filled with joy we couldn't give it. I wished it could tell me what we were missing.

"Yes. This is good." I meant that yes. With the ring back in Tyler's possession, my lungs filled more easily than they had in a week.

"Good," he repeated. "I think some people saw what you just gave me though so I need to get out of here. But we're good, and we're going to talk again soon?"

I assured him we were fine and he took his bible and left a mostly untouched cup of coffee on the table. I took a sip from mine and caught John staring at me. It appeared he was one of the people who had seen what I gave to Tyler. His older niece, Olivia, was sitting next to him chatting away and the younger one was carefully eating all the sprinkles off her donut. John left his coffee and donut between the girls and walked around a few laughing adults to reach my table.

There was one other person there, an older man who had turned a chair around to join the next table. John put his hand on Tyler's vacated chair and pulled it farther from me before he lowered himself into it.

"Are you..." He stuck his hand in his hair and knocked his glasses crooked. Rather than straighten them, he took them off and set them on the table. Then he sighed and put them back on. "Are you… okay?" His eyes combed my face with the strangest expression. It seemed he was afraid I might actually say something. But he'd just asked me a question.

"I'm fine," I said.

He nodded and stood up. Then he sat again. Someone that tall going up and down looked more fidgety than the average person. He took his glasses off and rubbed his face. Then he put them back on. Maybe it wasn't just his height. "Heidi," he said, "uh… are you sure you're okay?"

It was clear he wanted to ask me about giving the ring back but knew it would be better to ask Tyler. Tyler was his friend. I was nothing to him except through Tyler. But John would know soon enough anyway. "Yes, I'm sure," I said. "We didn't break up if you're hoping to finally be rid of me. We just decided to put the engagement on hold."

Pain flashed across his face when I accused him of hoping for a breakup, and I immediately regretted my words and the harsh tone. He must have thought he hid his dislike better. I knew I wasn't being fair. He couldn't control the way he felt about me – only the way he treated me – and he'd never been unkind or even disrespectful. I was the one watching too closely.

"Sorry," I mumbled. "Maybe I'm not completely fine."

"Heidi, I…" He swallowed hard and began digging at a chip in the table with his finger. "I don't…" He stopped himself and sent a plaintive look skyward. It seemed he couldn't even look at me. He began to shake his head and the frustration was evident. "You don't… or I can't…" He tapped his other hand against his knee a few times before he groaned and abruptly left. Not the table, the room. He didn't rejoin his sister's family. He left. He walked straight out the same door Tyler had left through. I was beginning to feel like a leper.

Monsignor Loy took the chair next. He liked to mingle and rarely stayed at a table long enough to sit. His posture said more to me than his smile. "You are having a difficult morning."

It was not a question. Either he'd been watching or my mental state was as plain as the sores of a leper. "I'm afraid I'm not very good company this morning."

~ 58 ~

"Have you had a donut?" he asked. "Sometimes a bite of something sweet is a tonic."

I shook my head. I wasn't in the mood for anything sweet. I didn't deserve a treat.

Monsignor Loy leaned a bit closer. "Remember that there is one who is always glad of our company. Even when we only feel like complaining, he listens with love."

The priest was a wise man. He delivered his advice without waiting for a response. If he'd stayed, I'd have simply told him I knew that. Or I'd have gotten defensive about my walk with God. But with no one there but myself, I was forced to admit that I'd become lazy with prayer. I hadn't put myself in God's company outside Sunday mornings in months.

I went home intending to remedy that. Being out of practice showed. I sat still and kept thinking God's name as though I needed to get his attention and then had nothing else to say. I tried a few Our Fathers, but lost my place more than once when my mind began to wander.

I took a break to start some laundry. The water shut off appropriately, and I stood there listening to the thrashing of my clothes. My mind overflowed with confusing thoughts. I let them spill out my mouth. The best way to pray might be to talk to myself and simply let God eavesdrop.

"What is wrong with me?" I said. "How can it feel wrong to be engaged and more wrong to be *un*engaged? This whole week has just been... wrong. I... there was that moment my hormones went wonky with John." I was staring at the washing machine and remembered him helping me fix it. "Okay, maybe there was more than one moment. But he doesn't matter. Tyler is... great. Why am I trying to screw it up? I let myself fret over that silly comment he made about a stranger being out of someone's league. I... we fought about something stupid. I've even been glad that baseball gives us an excuse to not talk. What changed? Why did we get along so well before he... Why were we so happy until he asked me to marry him? And why do I suddenly feel like I'm looking for reasons to find fault with a perfectly good man?"

My last words hit me hard. They crashed into my heart with an answer I did not want. I felt about Tyler the way I felt about my washing machine, which I gave a swift kick at the realization. I thought Tyler was a perfectly good man. And I was not in love with him. I didn't just have doubts. I knew there were things that made us incompatible and I was trying to fit him into my life anyway because he was a good man.

I didn't want to hurt his feelings, and I didn't want to take the risk that I wouldn't find someone better suited to me. I didn't want to break up because a breakup was always ugly and messy and I'd miss him. Tyler, and John by extension, was pretty much my entire social life. I may not be in love with him, but I honestly cared for him. I liked having him around, and I didn't want to give that up. While those were all fine reasons to be his friend, they were lousy reasons to get married. We couldn't get married. He was too serious for me. Money was of course a bigger issue, probably our biggest issue. He could do whatever he wanted with his money, but if it became our money, we'd spend the rest of our lives negotiating every purchase. I wasn't wrong to want him to save more. He wasn't wrong to want me to indulge a little more. We were different. We were not wrong, but we were wrong for each other. And most importantly, I didn't love him enough to overlook any of that.

I could make do with a can opener because it had no feelings. I knew that I would eventually decide I'd put up with enough, and it would go into the trash without another thought. I couldn't do that to Tyler. I couldn't simply discard a husband when I'd had enough. Being reminded where dating led had made me face that. And now I had to face the fact that if we couldn't get married, we shouldn't even be dating.

8

I talked to Tyler Monday morning more stimulated than if I'd had coffee. I was so afraid of betraying my decision over the phone. I owed him face to face. I think I managed to get through the brief call sounding natural. He was going to text me when he got off work. I should have enough time before John came over for the game to... do what I needed to do.

I didn't know exactly what I owed Tyler. I'd never broken up with anyone before. He was by far the longest relationship I'd had. I especially wasn't sure what to do about dinner. He expected me to bring something. I generally cooked at his place because he hated to cook and I'd rather cook than eat frozen dinners.

I knew that I needed to tell him right away. It had been hard enough not to blurt it out in the two-minute conversation we'd had that morning. What I really wanted was to suggest we change our status to friends and then enjoy a meal and a baseball game as though life was going to continue almost as before. But I wasn't nearly that naïve. That was against all the rules. And even though Tyler clearly had some doubts to have taken the ring back, that didn't mean he'd accept a complete end as peacefully as I had.

I couldn't plan on sticking around, but I was going to feel bad about leaving him to fend for himself for dinner at the last minute. Then there was John. I'd already forgiven myself for snapping at him Sunday morning, and I didn't feel bad about leaving *him* in the lurch about dinner, not when I thought about how happy he'd be to hear the news. It would be more awkward for Tyler though to have an extra person show up expecting food I hadn't made.

Then I got distracted by another problem. I was supposed to spend the afternoon with my grandparents. I wanted to see them. A nice walk sounded like a fun way to get my mind off the situation. Except that I knew it wouldn't work. I knew I couldn't spend time with them without fretting about what I was going to say to Tyler. Even if by some miracle no one in the family had told them about our engagement, they'd still ask how things were going with him.

It wouldn't feel right to talk through the end of the relationship before I'd actually ended the relationship. I texted Granddad that we'd have to postpone the visit because I wasn't feeling well. It felt like a lie even though it wasn't. I didn't say I was sick. I was jittery and anxious so I was definitely not feeling well. I would explain exactly what I meant when I saw them. He wished me a speedy recovery and told me to name a new date to get together as soon as I felt up to it.

I ended up preparing some cold ham sandwiches for Tyler and John. I stopped at the store for a bag of chips on my way to Tyler's apartment. Hoping for an excuse to delay going inside, I sat in the parking lot and checked my phone. A text from Kathy gave me what I wanted.

It said: `180 days!!!!`

I sent: `Till you get hitched? Cool.`

Then I sat back, waiting to see if she'd respond right away. My eyes took in Tyler's apartment building. They focused on the second floor, on Tyler's door. Was there any chance this wouldn't be the last time I knocked on that door?

I jumped at the text I was more or less expecting. Kathy sent several, almost as fast as I could read them.

`Yes!! I started the countdown at 200. Remember?`

`You should see my calendar. I have it all mapped out with deadlines and important dates.`

`100 days out is the anniversary of our first date. I love how that worked out!!`

I'm so excited! Don't know how I'll sleep
the next 180 days!
You need a countdown before I get to double
digits so we can track days together. Won't
that be fun?!!

I smiled at her enthusiasm in spite of my own situation. It
seemed that the idea of planning close weddings had grown on
her. It felt like the right moment to break the news to Kathy, as
though it might help me get used to it.
Doesn't look like I'm getting married
anytime soon. Keep it to yourself for now
though.

I sighed as I sent it, but it wasn't quite one of relief.
Is Tyler dragging his feet? What's his
problem?

Kathy didn't understand. I'd have to be blunt. I sent:
We're breaking up.

Kathy: What?!?! What happened?

Me: Nothing happened. We just aren't meant
to be.

Kathy: I'm sorry.

Me: Thanks. It's going to be okay.

I stared at my last line for a moment as I convinced myself it
was true. Then I put away the phone and got out of my car with
dinner in a grocery bag. I climbed the stairs feeling like someone
obviously about to make a run for it.

Tyler didn't notice that I brought something simple that
could be eaten any time and he didn't notice that I didn't have
any dishes I'd want back. He didn't notice the things I'd fretted
about. He did notice that I only brought two sandwiches, which
was one red flag that I somehow failed to spot.

"I guess Myrie's on his own tonight?" he said.

That's when I got less nervous about blurting and more
nervous about being able to get it out at all. "No, I... you can
eat with John."

"Oh." Tyler nodded. "Late lunch day?"

Sometimes when I didn't have to go to work or to church, I
slept in and had a late breakfast and a later lunch and skipped
dinner. "Yeah," I said. It wasn't why I didn't bring food for me,

but I did have a late lunch. "I mean, I... I don't think I'm going to stay for dinner tonight. Or the game."

Tyler looked puzzled as to why I came over without planning to stay but only for a moment. He set the food on his table and motioned me out of the kitchen. "Let's sit down."

I took my typical place on the loveseat, and he sat next to me for a change.

"I've been thinking," I said. "And praying. A lot. I've hardly done anything else since yesterday."

"And?" He looked like someone with a good idea what I was going to say, and that made it easier to say.

"And I don't think this... us... is going to work. I'm sorry."

He inhaled sharply as though perhaps he was surprised after all.

"You're great. I just—"

Tyler waved off my explanation.

I stopped hastily because I didn't want to give it.

"Heidi," he said, "after you handed me the ring so willingly yesterday, I... well... I suspected... I just thought it would take you longer."

He looked... not crushed. Disappointed, but not crushed. "So you're okay?"

"Not exactly. I mean, this sucks. But obviously, with this last week, I've been thinking and praying a lot about our future, too. I think I'm also realizing we're not... not perfect together. Besides I'm wondering if Myrie..." He shook his head at the mention of John as though he should not have brought him up.

And he shouldn't have. If Tyler had finally figured out that his friend didn't approve of me, it wasn't the best time to rub it in. I stood up. John wasn't due for another half hour, but I was suddenly panicky about him showing up early. "I should go now," I said.

Tyler nodded and walked me to the door. "Heidi, I hope... I'm not going to suggest we can still be friends because I know that's not how it works, but I hope we can at least be *friendly* if we run into each other."

"Of course. Next time you're at The Sleepy Crab, I'll only have them add a little extra mustard."

Tyler hated mustard. That was supposed to be a joke. He only smiled faintly.

I accepted it and said, "Goodbye."

I turned the music in my car much louder than usual to drive away unpleasant thoughts. It didn't work. I wiped a few tears from my cheeks as I walked up to my front door. Once I was inside, I grabbed a few tissues and curled up on my couch. I cried because my heart wasn't broken. I wanted to love someone, and I cried because I didn't. And I needed to mourn a change I hadn't planned for.

I called my mom after I was cried out and no longer sounded like I had a cold. She jumped right in with news of the family. Nothing major. One of my brothers was doing well in a summer soccer league. My youngest sister, age thirteen, had discovered a new series of books and Mom was having a hard time getting her to put it down long enough to eat.

When there was a pause, I tried to insert my news. "Mom, I have to tell you that you were right."

She laughed lightly. "Your mother is always right. What was I right about this time?"

"You were right that I wasn't excited about Tyler. We broke up."

"Oh, honey, I'm so sorry. I didn't want to be right about that."

"I know."

Mom mumbled something, and I realized she wasn't talking to me. She was probably filling in my dad. Then she said into the phone, "Do you need anything?"

"No. Don't worry about me, Mom. Even though I feel lousy right now, I think I already know this is one of those things I'll look back on and say was for the best."

"Is there anything I can do?"

"Like what, Mom?"

She chuckled at my sarcasm. "Like tell you that I believe you'll find the right guy soon and remind you that you're still a wonderful and well-loved person if you're single forever."

"Don't think that helps right now."

"Are you sure?" Mom asked. "I think I heard a smile."

Maybe she had. Maybe talking to someone who loved me did help. "Thanks, Mom. I'll talk to you again later." I hung up and checked to see if the Tigers were winning. I still wasn't a fan. I was just curious.

~~~~

It felt good to be back at work on Tuesday. Maggie noticed right away that I wasn't wearing a ring. When I told her why, she was shocked and appeared far more devastated than Tyler was when I told him. I worked until close, but it was a fairly quiet night. The most eventful thing was that Mr. and Mrs. Dewitt came in for dinner. They were the couple who owned the restaurant. And Mrs. Dewitt remembered my name. The good feeling that caused lasted only a moment because she also remembered that I had trained Griffin.

"I imagine my grandson has been here long enough to keep up without your help," she observed.

I nodded at her. She could imagine that if she wanted to.

"He doesn't talk about work much, but he's mentioned you."

"Really?" I hoped he hadn't mentioned me to his grandmother the way he mentioned me to me.

"I think he respects you." She tugged on the sleeve of her blouse when she said that. It seemed a deliberate ploy to avoid eye contact. I didn't know if she didn't quite believe what she was saying or only didn't want to see that I didn't believe it.

I tried to look pleased by the idea and not amused by it. I met the eyes of Mr. Dewitt as I asked what they'd like to order. The man wasn't much of a talker. In fact, I didn't think he'd ever said anything to me outside the name of a drink or food item. Probably a thank you or two as well. But he had kind eyes and they told me he knew at least a hint of what I wasn't saying about their grandson and didn't judge me for it. Perhaps Michelle had found a delicate way to report the friction between Griffin and the rest of the staff.

Griffin was standing by the door when I arrived on Wednesday. He smiled at me as he stepped on a cigarette.

"Haven't seen you in days," he said. "You been missing me this whole time?"

"Not the whole time."

He gave me an admiring look and then opened the door for me. He sighed when the pirate music started up right as we entered. I sang along, and he rolled his eyes as he walked away from me. It was another fairly quiet day. I mostly entertained myself by singing some yo ho hos whenever Griffin came up to try to bother me. There was one time I was sure he turned around extra fast so I wouldn't see him laugh. He was by the side door again when I left for the day.

He called out after I passed him. "It'd be easier on yourself if you just admitted you're in love with me."

I waved without turning around so he wouldn't see *me* laugh at that.

I got to work earlier on Thursday, which was great. I preferred the lunch shift. I like my regulars and we had more during lunch. "Good afternoon, everyone," I said to familiar faces. "How about one Coke, three Diet Cokes, two waters and," I zeroed in on Mr. Wildcard, "something the rest of us are missing out on?"

I received nods from most of the people around the table. Mr. Wildcard laughed. "I'm feeling like iced tea today with lots of lemon. Can you put like a whole lemon around the top of the glass?"

"I can. What if I got really crazy and mixed in one slice of lime?"

"Oh!" His eyebrows shot up. "You are a genius. Let's call this one... Delight of My Life."

Lots of his coworkers groaned right along with me.

"What?" he said.

"We just know you can do better." I bit back a smile as the woman next to him shook her head vigorously at my diplomacy. "I'll bring the drinks right out."

I filled up the glasses and arranged the fruit-topped one for Mr. Wildcard. I was picking up the tray when the hostess darted into the kitchen. "Heidi, I just seated twenty-one," she said. "He asked for you special and he was here yesterday, too." She winked at me before she disappeared again.

My eyes searched out table twenty-one as I reentered the dining room. It was John Myrie. Alone. He asked for me? What was that all about? He could avoid me easily enough now that Tyler and I were through and he was looking for me? Nerves in my chest tingled a warning, but I had work to do before I could face John.

"Water," I said as I set down the first glass. "This is the regular Coke." I continued around the table, setting down the iced tea last.

"It's a work of art," Mr. Wildcard said.

"A work of art with a dumb name." The coworker who looked youngest narrowed his eyes disapprovingly at the glass.

"Nonsense." Mr. Wildcard ran his hand around the side of the glass. "This *is* the delight of my life. At this moment."

"Are you ready to order?"

They were. I jotted everything down and ignored the fluttering in my chest as I walked up to John. "Hi," I said. "Welcome to The Sleepy Crab. Have you been here before?"

He smiled at my joke and that flutter began to knock against my ribs. "Once or twice," he said.

"What can I get you to drink?"

"Water."

I nodded firmly and moved away. Be professional, I reminded myself. John was there to eat, not to talk. But if that was the case, why had he asked for me?

I entered the last order into the computer before I got John's drink and Griffin appeared beside me. "Heidi, if you undress me with those eyes one more time, my clothes might actually come off."

"Would that be so bad?"

"Not for the ladies here, but some of the guys might be jealous."

Even with our new repartee, I had no response for that.

Griffin moved into my line of sight. "I suppose it would give you some new material for your fantasies."

"Thanks," I said, "but I don't need any more."

"Very good." He wiggled his eyebrows and left me alone.

I brought out a glass of water with a few steadying breaths. "Here you are." I flipped a coaster out of my apron and set the glass in front of John. "Do you know what you want for lunch?"

"I, um… How are you?"

He looked uncertain and the scene felt uncomfortably familiar as I said, "I'm fine."

He sort of studied me for a moment. I thought he was about to ask me something, but he said, "Macaroni and cheese."

I wrote it down. "My favorite."

"I know."

I meant to offer only a small smile at his acknowledgment. There was something in his eyes when I looked up though, something that seemed to say he knew a lot more than what food I liked, something that said he knew *me*. I reminded myself that he did know me, and he didn't like what he knew. "It'll be ready in two shakes of a lamb's tail."

I got that expression from my dad. It never got a reaction from Tyler. John looked as amused as usual, and it felt genuine. Most of the time he did a good job hiding his disdain for me. I tried to be grateful for that. He didn't say anything else to me while he was there, at least nothing that wasn't related to having lunch in a restaurant. But when I cleared his table, he'd left both copies of the receipt. On the back of his, he'd written, "I'm sorry, Heidi. I didn't want to want this."

I folded it up and put it in my pocket where it weighed heavily on me through the afternoon. I began to wonder if I had misjudged John's disapproval. It looked different in light of my own new perspective. Maybe he didn't have anything against me personally and had only figured out sooner than I did that I wasn't a good match for Tyler. Maybe he'd seen the two of us would eventually make each other miserable. I could understand now how that could be hard to watch. Was he being nice now because he was afraid he'd driven something between us or inadvertently said something to Tyler to hasten the breakup? Or did he just feel guilty for being right?

John was not at fault though, and it made me so mad that I couldn't blame him. I wanted him to be a horrible person because he'd rejected me. I didn't want to admit John made me feel anything anymore, and I tried to spend as little time as possible thinking about any of that.

I concentrated on work as the place began to fill for dinner. I waited on a small group of women I recognized from church. One of them offered to give me a hundred dollars if I would turn off the music. I told her I couldn't take her money even if the music was my call, but that I could probably get it turned down for her.

Griffin caught me with my hand on the volume. "I knew it," he said. "You hate it, too."

I sang, "Swabbing the deck and swashing my buckles, looking for gems and pearls and opals." It was the most ridiculous of all the songs.

He grunted and turned away. Then he quickly turned back with his hand out.

"What?"

"I know you're secretly blowing kisses at me. I was trying to catch one."

"You won't," I said. "I'm good with secrets."

"You're good with a lot of things." It was a different male voice that responded. A server named Peter had inserted himself into our conversation. He was talking to me, but his eyes were on Griffin in a way that suggested he'd made the comment only to imply the opposite about him. Griffin laughed as though he didn't care and walked away.

I mumbled a thanks to Peter in case he also meant the compliment, then I went out to greet a pair of new customers. It was a man who looked around fifty with a woman who might have been close to my age. I felt myself hoping she wasn't his date, even if it wasn't my business. "Good evening," I said. "Welcome to The Sleepy Crab. Can I start you with something to drink?"

"Water," the woman said.

The man looked me up and down. "Hello," he said. His tone made me feel as though I'd forgotten to put on clothes. "Aren't you going to make this a wonderful dinner?"

"I'll do my best, sir. Do you know what you'd like to drink?"

"I'm afraid I forgot everything the moment you walked up."

I tried to make a sigh look like a simple weight shift. "Shall I come back?"

"I'm sure that won't be necessary." The woman spoke sharply with her eyes locked on the man across from her.

He glanced that way but kept his focus on me. "What do you recommend?"

"Something thirst-quenching."

He smiled as though I'd said something suggestive. "Water will do," he said.

"Do you need a minute before you order?"

"If it means watching you walk away an extra time."

The woman shot daggers at him from her eyes, and he didn't appear to notice. I smiled at her. "I'll just give you a minute while I get the drinks."

That was a difficult table. The man paid me too much attention and continued to serve up smarmy compliments. When I tried to set their check on the table, he clasped it and my hand between his unusually beefy paws. The uninvited touch made me very glad I was nearing the end of my shift.

Unfortunately, the inappropriate man and his companion finished around the same time I did. I cleared their table just before I took off my apron and clocked out. When I went out the side door, I saw the man standing in the parking lot with his phone pressed to his ear. The woman – possibly his daughter – must have been sitting in a nearby car waiting for him to hang up.

"Hello!" His voice sounded a little too delighted to see me. "What was your name again?" He put his phone in his pocket as he walked towards me, and though it was still daylight and I wasn't afraid, I took a few steps as I said my name. I walked away from my car and placed myself in front of the large side window where people could see us through the glass.

"Thanks again for such excellent service," he said. "Can I get a quick hug before I go?"

"Thank you, sir. But I'm not a hugger."

"Aw. Just a quick one." He reached out an arm.

"Hey!" Griffin came charging at us out of nowhere holding an as yet unlit cigarette. "I heard her tell you to back off from over there," he said. "What's wrong with your ears?" He wrapped his arm around my waist in a gesture that felt shockingly protective.

~ 71 ~

The man had already backed up. He held his hands out defensively. "Only trying to show my appreciation for your woman." He kept his eyes on Griffin for a minute as he made his way towards his car.

Griffin's arm let go of me as I realized I had let myself lean into him. He bumped his eyebrows up and down. "He called you my woman. I bet you liked the sound of that."

Just when I'd seen a glimmer of a gentleman. I struggled against giving him the satisfaction of a scowl. "You never turn it off, do you?"

"My charm? It doesn't have an off switch. Sorry it's too much for you." He walked away lighting his cigarette.

"Griffin?"

"Yeah?" He didn't look back.

"Thank you."

He just waved over his shoulder.

9

My hairdryer shorted out more than once Friday morning. I planned to braid my hair though and if I didn't get it dry first, it'd still be damp at the end of the day. I gave the dryer a good whack to keep it going.

Maggie worked the lunch shift with me. Her bright smile seemed slightly dented by my newly single status. Several times she grinned at me and then reigned it in as she apparently remembered that I might be in mourning or something. I'd been thinking all week about what to do about the new gap in my social life, and I got an idea that could help me and assure Maggie that I'd already done all the crying I needed. I found her in the kitchen during the quiet time mid-afternoon.

"Hey, Maggie, are you busy tonight?"

"Of course not. Another Friday night with my parents."

"Do you want to maybe do something with me?"

"Awesome!" No teeth missing from the smile. "What do you want to do?"

"I just thought you could come over and do like a girls' movie night. Would that be fun?"

"Yes. That would be so great. Can I bring the popcorn?" Her expression would have likely been exactly the same if I had asked her to come to Disney World with me.

"What's your number?" I pulled out my phone. "I'll text you my address and you can come over as soon as you're ready."

"Yea!" Maggie bounced while we traded some information. She recovered her usual brightness through the early dinner customers and said she'd see me soon as we left for the day.

I had a small stack of DVDs on the table for Maggie to choose from when she arrived. "Do you want a tour of my place first?" I asked her.

"Sure."

"Okay. Stand right here."

She followed my instruction.

"That's the kitchen. Turn a little bit this way. Now you're facing the living room. Little more. Through that door's the bedroom." I had actually made my bed once I knew I was expecting company. "That's the bathroom," I said. "And now we turn back to the kitchen."

"It's awesome," Maggie said. She handed me a shopping bag. "I brought M&Ms, too."

"Oh. M&Ms and popcorn. Good combo."

She grinned at the compliment. I told her to pick a movie while I got the popcorn in the microwave.

"I haven't seen this one." She held up a case. "Is it okay with you?"

Since the movies were all favorites that people bought me because they knew they were favorites, I'd have been okay with any of them. We got it started as soon as our snacks were ready. Maggie and I laughed at the same lines, and she looked excited to see that. I think the shared time was healthier for me than the popcorn and M&M dinner. I didn't need to ask if she liked the movie, but I did. We talked for quite a while after it ended. First about the movie then we drifted through a few other topics. Eventually she asked me how much longer I thought Griffin was going to last at The Sleepy Crab.

"I don't know," I said. "I think Michelle might cave on the pirate music first."

"I know. She was so funny the other day when she talked about hearing that one song in the middle of a dream."

I tried to imitate our boss. "I am not kidding. I woke up wanting to punch my husband and he hadn't even done anything."

Maggie laughed. "That is the worst song."

"Maybe Michelle could edit the loop to skip that one."

"Or maybe Griffin could just quit. He is so onerous. Do you like that word? I like onerous and I don't get to use it much, but it definitely describes Griffin."

"I don't know," I said. "Sometimes I think he's not so bad."

"Really?" Maggie looked down for a minute. "You wouldn't... I mean, would you actually go out with him?"

"No way." I held up a couch pillow as though I was going to chuck it at her for suggesting such a thing.

"But you just said—"

"I know what I said. I'm not interested in casual dating though and there's a huge difference between not so bad and potential husband. Besides, he's six years younger than I am. Don't you think that'd be weird?"

Maggie shot me a teasing smile. "He does have a rich family and a trust fund."

"I should reconsider then. He *is* cute."

"Are you kidding?"

"About trying to marry him for his money? Of course. About the other thing? He's really not bad looking, but I think he'd look better with a normal hair color."

"So you wouldn't make fun of me if I said I thought so, too?" Her slightly embarrassed expression as Maggie made her admission suddenly made me feel sort of old.

"No," I said. "I'd only make fun of you if you said his personality was attractive. Although he does have his moments." I told her how he scared off the customer who tried to hug me.

"So he is capable of being nice." Maggie thoughtfully twisted an empty glass in her hand. "Why do you think he doesn't try harder?"

"Who knows?" It was an interesting question though. "Maybe he doesn't have an incentive, like a strong faith in God. Maybe he's spent his whole life having people try to be his friend for his money and pushes everyone away as a defense mechanism. And maybe," I smiled at Maggie, "he just enjoys being *onerous*."

She grinned at my use of the word then it faded a little. "I suppose you won't be dating anyone for a while anyway."

~ 75 ~

"I don't know that either," I said. "I guess it depends when I meet someone."

"But you can't... I mean, wouldn't you feel awful if Tyler started dating someone else right away?"

Would I? "I don't think so. If I was still in love with him, I'd be jealous to see him with someone else. But we broke up at least partly because we weren't in love."

"I guess that makes sense. You're really not heartbroken?"

"I'm upset that it didn't work and if you want to know the truth, I'm kind of embarrassed that it took me so long to figure that out. I suppose someday I'll look back and think a year wasn't that long, but right now I feel bad for wasting Tyler's time."

"Hmm..." Maggie looked doubtful. A year probably seemed even longer to her than it did to me. She sighed. "Speaking of time, I should get going. It's after eleven and," she paused to roll her eyes, "my parents still wait up for me."

"All right." I stood up to clear away our dishes. "But we should do this again."

She grinned and nodded enthusiastically. "Yes, definitely." She thanked me several times before I closed the door on her.

~~~~

The restaurant was extra busy on Saturday. I don't know what caused it, but I wasn't complaining about rushing around. I stayed later than usual as the stragglers had to be reminded that we all wanted to go home eventually.

I hit snooze in the morning and contemplated shutting the alarm off altogether. I didn't have to work so I could go to the later mass after coffee and donuts. I could skip coffee, too. The realization that I'd have coffee alone somehow woke me up. That wouldn't necessarily be the case. I might be able to find someone new to sit with. That seemed more likely if I came in at the start, right after the early mass. I got out of bed and began to get ready.

I sat alone in church, which I didn't mind because that was normal. I walked out and my eyes sadly traveled the familiar path to the bench where Tyler had always waited for me. John was there. John was there alone where he used to wait with Tyler. He stood up when he saw me. "Good morning, Heidi."

I blinked at the unexpected appearance. "Uh... hi."

"Can I walk with you?" He motioned towards the parish hall.

I sort of nodded as we began to move with the crowd. It was a quiet walk. People were chatting and laughing around us, but neither John nor I said anything. We got in line for coffee. John didn't join his sister, though he waved at his nieces as he passed them. He filled a cup, added a splash of cream, and handed it to me without a word.

He filled a cup for himself and led me to some empty seats. I took one of them, thinking about the note he left at The Sleepy Crab and the fact that I hadn't thrown it away. It was safer to think about the note itself. John might be here now looking for a response.

"How are you?" he asked.

"Fine."

"Good morning, my sheep." Monsignor Loy was next to us, and I hadn't seen him approach.

"Good morning," I said, not minding the interruption at all. John's surprising appearance was still confusing me.

"And I might say the same to you? Soon?" The priest was giving John a strangely hopeful look.

"Maybe." John wasn't coy, more contemplative.

Monsignor Loy nodded and winked at me as he moved to greet someone else.

I wanted to ask John what had just happened, but when I looked back at him, he said, "How are you?"

I said, "Fine." We'd had this conversation a few times already.

John shook his head. "I'm not making small talk, Heidi. I want to know how you're doing. Even if it's none of my business."

"All right. I'm disappointed, and I do miss Tyler but I'm not drowning in heartache and it's okay if you tell me that he's not either. This was... for the best." My leg was jumping nervously under the table. I didn't know why I was telling John something that really wasn't his business.

"I'm sorry that you think…" He set his cup down and seemed to be wrestling with words in his head while his hands went from the table to his lap and back to the table. "Heidi, I know you saw through me, but you saw the wrong thing."

"It's okay," I said. I think my voice betrayed the fact that it wasn't okay, at least not yet. I was trying not to be mad at John for seeing what I didn't see, but it made me feel foolish and that was prompting a little misdirected anger. "I understand now."

"I don't think you… you *don't* understand." John's expression made me worry that he was about to tell me something awful. But if he hadn't been secretly hating my guts – and there was no reason to tell me that now that he could easily avoid me – I was at a loss.

An interruption appeared at his elbow in the form of a small blond child. Her eyes seemed as big as the donut she held out to him. "You forgot a donut, Uncle John."

"Oh. Thanks, sweetheart."

She turned those eyes on me as John took the plate she offered. "Mommy said I should ask if you want one, too."

She looked eager to get me one so I agreed. I watched her run to the dessert table and back to me with a chocolate covered donut on a small white plate.

"Thank you," I said.

She beamed and ran back to her family. I looked at John to see if he was going to spit out whatever he wanted to say to me. The fingers of one hand were on the side of the donut plate in front of him. His other elbow was resting on the table with his hand in his hair as he watched Olivia. He apparently wasn't going to talk if she was coming back.

Olivia picked up her plate and cup of water. She said something to her mom before she rushed back to me and John like someone on an important mission. She plunked her treat on the table between us – in the spot Tyler could have had – and climbed onto the chair. I assumed she had business with her uncle, but she essentially turned her back on him.

"I'm Olivia," she said to me. "What's your name?"

"I'm Heidi."

"Are you Uncle John's friend?"

It was a lot more complicated to me but to a five-year-old, a friend was someone who was currently trying to be nice to you so I nodded at her.

"You're pretty," she said.

"Thank you."

"Do you have a cat?"

"No. I don't have any pets."

"I want a cat." She took a bite of donut and kept talking. "Mommy says I'm too little. She says maybe I can have one when I'm eight."

When some of my siblings begged for a pet, my mom suggested they might get one at a time far enough in the future that she hoped they'd forget. It had worked both times. I wondered if Kim was trying the same tactic. "What would you name a cat if you had one?"

"I want a white one," Olivia said. "I'd name her Elsa."

"What if it was a boy?"

She gave me a funny look. "All cats are girls."

"Oh." I tried to look as though I'd merely forgotten that obvious fact. "Are you excited about having a new baby brother?"

Olivia smiled as she nodded. "I get to stay with Uncle John when he's born."

I took the chance to include John in the conversation. "You're on call for babysitting?"

"Yeah." He put down the coffee he'd been about to drink. "I told Kim she needs to plan her labor better this time though. When Kate was born, they dropped this one with me at 3 o'clock in the morning."

"I'm sure she did that just to annoy you."

He shrugged with an expression that said he wouldn't put it past her.

I looked back at Olivia. "Do you like staying with your uncle?"

"Oh, yes." She leaned forward as though she was about to tell me a vital secret. "He has *Princess* Candy Land."

I almost smiled at the picture in my head of John playing with this little girl. Almost. It was too close to a mushy spot in my heart. "That sounds fun," I said.

~ 79 ~

"Can you come over and play with us?" Her eyes widened again.

"Uh…" I glanced at John. He took that moment to decide he was very hungry for the donut Olivia had brought him. I gave her the most non-committal answer I knew. "We'll see."

"You can be Rapunzel," she said. "I like Cinderella and Uncle John has to be Ariel."

That was just too cute. I held back the laugh. "You *have* to be Ariel?"

He didn't look remotely embarrassed. He nodded to Olivia and said, "Tell her why."

"Why what?" she asked.

"Tell her why you decided I had to play with Ariel."

"Oh. Because you have brown hair." Her tone was matter-of-fact and John gave me a somewhat helpless look to indicate he had no way to argue with logic he did not understand. If he tried, it might have done as much good as pointing out to her that no one said I'd be playing the game.

Olivia snuck in a few more questions as she finished her donut. Then Kim showed up to reclaim her daughter. I thought there might be an awkward moment since the last time I talked to her, she was congratulating me on an engagement that had since ended. She simply gave me a friendly greeting before she took her daughter by the hand. "Come on, honey," she said. "You've spent enough time with Uncle John. We're going to let him talk to Heidi now."

The little girl didn't pout. She waved happily at me as she was led away. John tried to wave at her, too, but she didn't seem to notice him. "I think you have a new fan," he said.

"She's adorable." I watched her return to her family and begin chatting at her dad. When I turned back to John, he was looking at me.

I remembered that there might be a reason he was sitting with me. I took a sip of my coffee. It sat in my mouth an extra moment while I reminded myself how to swallow. The people around us swirled into a single background image as John slid forward to take the chair Olivia had vacated. I was too warm. Curiosity about what he wanted was burning a hole in my stomach. The fear though… it was more powerful. I was afraid if I stayed where I was he would see that I was too warm.

"I guess I'll head for home," I said, forcing nonchalance I didn't feel, pretending Olivia had made me forget she had interrupted something.

John opened his mouth and closed it again as I stood.

"I… uh…" I wanted to say something like *I'll see you later*, but I had no idea if that was true. I said only, "Bye."

I made my way through the building to wave at Monsignor Loy before I left. Then I tossed my cup in a trash can by the door and stepped into the bright sunshine of a summer day. There were flowering trees along the sidewalk, the scent of coffee followed me from the parish hall, and a little boy was laughing hysterically on his dad's shoulders. The idyllic scene was marred by the feeling that I was running away from something and by the uneasiness of not knowing what it was.

I rounded the corner of the building and was about to cut into the parking lot when a side door opened and John came through it. There was no more doubt he intended to head me off than there was that I wanted to let him. Some unseen force pulled me right towards him even though my mind was screaming at me that the encounter would not end well.

"Did I forget something?" I asked. Perhaps there was a practical reason he tried to catch me.

"Heidi… will you let me explain something?"

I nodded mutely, waiting to get it over with.

"Did Tyler ever tell you that… that we, uh… why I left Sacred Heart?" John looked puzzled by his last words. I got the distinct impression that wasn't the way he had intended to end that sentence.

"No," I said, wanting to know if there was something Tyler didn't tell me and wondering if John and I were about to discuss the price of eggs in China instead.

"It was a girl." He lifted one shoulder to accentuate the glib tone. "I dated someone when I was in college who went to Thompsonville Christian," he gave a nod towards Sacred Heart as he talked, presumably to indicate the building on the other side of it, "and it didn't last long – me and her – and I was too… I didn't want her or my parents or anyone else to know she was the only reason I left here. So I stuck with Thompsonville Christian until it kind of became a habit."

He sounded almost like he was confessing something so I tried to respond carefully. "I don't know that you can say going to church is a *bad* habit."

"No, I…" John reached up and plucked a handful of tiny white blooms from a branch. He absently began to separate and drop the petals between his fingers. "It's just that I always sort of thought I'd eventually rejoin my family here. I thought if I waited long enough it'd look like a new decision and not a reevaluation of a hasty one. So it's funny now that… I mean, that I wouldn't care if…" He dropped his eyes to the tiny white flecks on the sidewalk.

My mind was a jumble of thoughts. He'd clearly followed me out to talk about something specific. I knew we weren't talking about whatever that was, and I wanted to know why. Why, if he didn't dislike me as I'd long assumed, did it still feel as though there was something wrong between us? Why did it feel as though we were on the verge of an argument? Why couldn't I bring myself to just ask what was going on? And why in the name of everything that has ever not made sense was I staring so fixedly at his mouth while I waited for him to say something else?

I immediately began to study the flower remnants on the ground as well.

John said, "So how much do you really hate baseball?"

His shift to teasing startled a smile out of me. "I don't hate baseball."

"Are you sure? I can tell you don't… or that you hadn't been… pretending to like it as much as you used to."

"I never pretended. I just… well, Tyler's enthusiasm was kind of infectious in the beginning, but it never fully… just because I'm not as excited as some people doesn't mean I'm not enjoying it at all."

John raised his eyebrows skeptically, sort of like he *wanted* to believe me.

"I do like baseball. It's just that I can't bring myself to care so much about who wins."

"That's blasphemy," he said, shaking his head slowly.

"I wish I could go to a game in person sometime."

"Hey, that'd be, um… you should." His face had lit up for a second with what I thought was the idea of taking me to a game. Then he seemed to realize I might read something into that. Or Tyler might. Which did John think would be worse?

"You went to a Tigers game a while back, right? When you were visiting family?"

"Yeah. It was great. Nosebleed seats of course, but it didn't matter because the right team won." He said it seriously, but his eyes expected me to laugh and I obliged. "Have you seen that guy – I can't remember his name, the one who comes to the restaurant and says your name a lot – have you seen him lately?"

"He was in yesterday actually, which was kind of weird because I thought he'd only ever been in for weekday lunches. Why do you ask?"

"I don't know." John shrugged at the same time. "I just like the way you can impersonate him without sounding like you're mocking him."

"He *is* funny. Yesterday when I said I was surprised to see him he said, 'I like Saturdays, Heidi. Heidi, I like this place, too. You should only be surprised when you don't see me.' Then he ordered the fish sandwich – like always – and asked if I was surprised."

John laughed with me and I tried to relax.

"Did, um… did you make it to the art museum on Monday?" he asked.

"No. I bowed out because… I guess because I needed time alone to think." I didn't really want to bring up what happened on Monday, but I figured it wouldn't hurt. John already knew. That may have been why he asked if I made it and not how it was.

"Have you rescheduled the trip?"

"Not yet." Granddad hadn't texted me since he said I should name a new day when I was feeling better. I couldn't – or didn't want to – explain why I was dragging my feet.

"You want to go, don't you?"

"Yeah… I was trying to remember exactly how long it's been since I was there."

"I think it was early October," John said.

~ 83 ~

That's what I'd been starting to think. "You remember that?"

"Sure. You were going on and on about it."

"Oh, right. You and Tyler were trying to watch a playoff game, weren't you?"

"Oh, I didn't…" John nudged his glasses while the dark eyes behind them softened apologetically. "I didn't mean *on and on* in a bad way. It sounded like you had a lot more fun than I've ever had at an art museum."

"Maybe." I kicked self-consciously at the edge of the grass.

"Are you worried they don't want to see you as much as you want to see them?"

I kept my eyes on the toe of my shoe as it flattened a few unsuspecting blades of green. I couldn't let him see that he was right. How did he know what I didn't say?

"They want to see you, Heidi," John said gently. "Don't make them beg."

We were talking about me a lot. I wanted to talk about something else. "How's the new guy working out?"

"Huh?"

"Didn't you say you had a new guy at work a few weeks ago?"

"Oh, yeah. He seems quiet and competent. I gotta say those are good traits in a coworker."

"So I guess that means he's working out."

"As far as I'm concerned. I suppose you've never worried about that because you don't worry about anything unless you decide to."

"You think I decide to worry?"

"No. You decide *not* to worry. Like with Griffin. When he started you were like, 'I hear the owners' grandson is a piece of work, but I won't let him get to me.' And then you didn't. You'd repeat things he said to you like you were impressed with the amount of effort he wasted trying to annoy you. Meanwhile, it kind of made me want to go let the air out of his tires."

"I knew the second time he suggested I'd get better tips if I started flashing customers that he'd run out of ideas. And you wouldn't really do that."

"You don't think I would?"

"No. You're nicer than that."

"Am I?" John looked at me searchingly, as though my limp compliment was surprisingly high praise. I squirmed to know that from me it was. I'd wanted to hate him for rejecting me and felt justified when the feeling was mutual. It appeared that not only did he know about the animosity I'd manufactured, but he also knew that I'd recognized my mistake. Was I a complete open book to him? I didn't read censure in his eyes, but if I'd been wrong about the dread I'd seen for months, maybe I was wrong now. One thing I did know was that I hoped at least some of my pages were written in invisible ink.

"Of course you're nice," I said, shifting under the weight of my own guilt more than any perceived interrogation. "Olivia thinks so and she seems pretty smart."

He smiled. "You know she also thinks I work for Santa Claus."

"What? She doesn't really think that, does she?"

"She does."

"Why would you tell her that?"

John put his hands up defensively while he laughed. "It wasn't me. Kim said she asked about my job and she didn't want to scare her with how boring it really is so she said I worked for Santa, that I work on a program that helps him keep up when kids move. I tried to tell Olivia the truth, but Kim had told her that I'd have to deny it because keeping the secret was part of my job."

"Wait a minute. Did you tell Santa I moved? Is that why I didn't get a plant last year?"

John laughed, but then he said, "Did you really want a plant?"

I chose to focus on the slightly teasing tone of his voice that said a plant was a strange thing to want. My mind wanted to go a few other places though. It tried to tell me the squint behind his glasses might mean he'd have gotten me one if he'd known. It tried to remind me that Tyler had known, and he gave me a pretty but unnecessary bracelet. I wore it the Sunday after Christmas and possibly one other time. I'd sort of forgotten I had it. Then I shut my mind down before it could tell me there was any hope of a gift from John next year. Christmas was six months away. He'd have completely worked through any guilty feelings causing him to be nice to me long before that.

"Yes, I wanted a plant," I said. "I'd like to have something easier than a pet to take care of and… I don't know why, but I feel like I'd be more attached to a plant if someone gave it to me."

"I guess that's not that weird."

"Not *that* weird." I narrowed my eyes at him.

"It's not weird at all for you. You've decided it should be a gift. There's no looking back."

"What is that supposed to mean?" I thought we were having a frivolous conversation and something about his comment struck a deeper, more personal chord.

"Relax, Heidi. That's a good thing. I love how crazy determined you are. That's why I wanted to come over when you tackled your washing machine. I knew you were going to fix it if you had to learn to disassemble the whole thing."

I shrugged uncomfortably at his exaggeration, but John wasn't looking for a response. He kept talking, trying to convince me of something about myself.

"Do you remember the peanut butter? I bet you don't. We were at Tyler's for a baseball game. It was one of the last times you let him cook." His fingers came up in air quotes. "You'd made him promise it wouldn't be anything that involved a freezer and a plastic tray and he made peanut butter sandwiches. He was about to open a new jar and you told him the other one wasn't empty yet. And you proved it. I have never seen anyone scrape out a peanut butter jar with more determination. Tyler said it was an awful lot of work for a sandwich, and I think he wanted to say you were just cheap and yeah, let's not pretend that isn't part of it." He smiled, more to himself. "But it's more that you don't want to give up on anything until you're ready. Because it isn't always about money. You just decide something and that's it. Like that guy you work with again. When you started talking about how obnoxious he was, you didn't complain about him because you'd already decided he wouldn't bother you. You just *decided* not to be bothered. That's amazing. And now you've decided a plant is better from someone else. I wish you could…"

The church bells had started ringing while he was talking and he looked startled, as though they'd woken him up. "I, uh… I have to go," he said. He looked at Sacred Heart and some people rushing into the side door. "I still need to… I overslept so I need to go to church." He ran his hand through his hair with something like frustration as he glanced back at me. "Bye, Heidi."

"Bye." I waved.

John glanced back a few times, looking reluctant as he walked away. We had apparently never made it back to the topic he wanted to discuss. If he hadn't been to church, John hadn't simply stopped at that bench on his way home. He'd come early. He'd come early looking for me.

I moved quickly to my car to outrun a thought. It chased me. What if Tyler sent him? What if he kept asking how I was because Tyler wasn't as okay with the situation as he'd seemed to me? What if John was looking for signs I'd restart something with Tyler? If he thought there was any chance we'd get back together, that would explain why he hadn't come right out and said he knew we were a bad idea.

My feelings about all that were way too complicated to begin to untangle. It was so much easier to remain confused and in denial.

10

The Sleepy Crab greeted me with its usual sights and sounds. The boats in the funky frames on the walls hadn't changed in all the time I'd worked there. The music was sort of new and only temporary, but familiar enough that I was happy to hear it. Happy to throw myself into the routines of my job. I'd been doing pretty well thinking only mundane thoughts since I got home from church the day before. Having work to focus on would make that easier.

My first customer was the funny guy who liked my name so much. "Hi, James. Welcome back to The Sleepy Crab."

"Heidi. Heidi, good to see you."

"What would you like to start with?" I asked, as if I didn't know.

His lips mashed a smile before it could show fully. "Dr. Pepper. Maybe."

"Maybe?"

"Heidi. Heidi, I don't know." He looked at the door then lowered his voice. "I'm meeting someone. Is it bad if I order a drink without her?"

"No." I shook my head to emphasize that. "I think she'd expect that. And I can catch her up quick as soon as she gets here."

"Okay."

"So… Dr. Pepper?"

"Yeah. Thanks, Heidi. Heidi, you're great."

"Thank you for saying I'm great." Just great, nothing that made me think.

His smile was on me, but his eyes were back on the door, then on the table, then on one of those boat pictures. He was still alone when I brought his drink, even with a delay on my part. I set it in front of him. "Don't worry," I said. "I'll keep my eye on you so I know when you need me again."

I did just that while I greeted a few women at a nearby table. Michelle, the manager, was doing hostess duty for lunch and she seated a familiar group for me next.

"Hello, gentlemen. Bad news. I'm afraid we're out of shrimp tacos today."

All three of them laughed, but one of them more quietly than the others. "You are kidding, right?" he asked me.

"Yes, I am."

He put his hand over his heart. "It is not nice to scare people like that."

"Sorry. How about I sneak in an extra shrimp to make up for it?"

"Then all is forgiven."

I took his friends' orders and ducked into the kitchen. Maggie was sitting next to the drink machine while I filled some glasses, her arms folded across her chest. "You all right?" I asked.

"I'm just bored and feeling unloved, that's all."

Unloved? My mind poked me with a thought that someone might not be unloved. But I was trying not to think about him. Maggie. I was talking to Maggie and only thinking about Maggie. "Why are you bored and unloved?"

"I only have one table because the last three people all asked for someone specific. Not me."

"You know you have your regulars, too."

"Yeah." She flashed her toothy smile. "I'm sure they'll all be here tomorrow."

I delivered a few drinks and my table of women still appeared engrossed in their menus so I decided to check on James.

"Hi. Any word from your friend?"

"Heidi... Heidi..." He winced at me before his eyes traveled over and around the phone on the table. "She's not coming."

"I'm sorry. Are you still staying for lunch?"

"It's not like I don't eat alone all the time. Can I have the fish sandwich?"

"Absolutely." The guy's expression reminded me of Maggie's in the kitchen and that gave me an idea. "Hey, James, how would you feel about some temporary company?"

"Aren't you busy?" His posture perked up a bit.

"*I* am... but don't go anywhere."

He laughed nervously as I slipped away from his table. "Maggie!" I waved at her to hurry out of the kitchen. She followed me looking confused.

"James, this is Maggie. She was just telling me how bored she was. Do you mind if she sits with you... just until your food is ready?"

"Not at all, Heidi. Heidi, that's a great idea."

Maggie shot me a wide-eyed look over her shoulder as she sat down. It was too quick to determine if it was excitement or panic. I was sure to find out one way or the other soon enough. I explained the situation to Michelle, who gave her eager approval. Standing someone up was not okay with her. The women I'd given drinks some time ago were all still studying their menus. I stopped by to see if they had any questions.

One of them appeared about my age and maybe ten years younger than her companions. She looked at me over the top of her menu. "This bacon burger," she said, "it's not a hamburger topped with bacon, but a whole burger made out of bacon?"

"Oh, yeah. It smells better than anything else that comes from the kitchen. Except maybe a couple of desserts."

"Is it, like, a guy sandwich?"

"It does seem popular with guys, especially younger ones."

She sighed and said, "Well, I guess..."

Another woman at the table spoke up. "Is that what's taking so long? You don't want to order a *guy* sandwich?"

"No. Or... it sounds so good, but I don't think I could eat it all."

The woman who asked her rolled her eyes as though she didn't believe the response.

But the third woman said, "Hey! I'll split it with you."

The young one brightened. "Will you get a salad if I get the bacon burger and we'll give each other half?" She looked at me when she got her nod.

"Do you want me to split those in the kitchen? I can bring you each a plate with half a burger and half a salad."

"That'd be great. Thanks."

The last woman got the shrimp tacos. Those seemed to be popular with everyone.

I had two orders ready at the same time. One was James' sandwich and I'd just seen Maggie giving him that impossible to resist smile so I grabbed the other one first.

"Here we are, gentlemen. I had to arm-wrestle some guy in the kitchen and promise my firstborn to someone else to get that extra shrimp on there so I hope the tacos are *really* tasty today." I felt good as I put the food down amidst their laughter. Tips were wonderful, but I'd take these smiles over an extra dollar.

"I bet you don't even weigh a hundred pounds. Whoever you arm-wrestled must be tiny."

We all knew I was kidding anyway so I thought I might as well up the ante. I raked my eyes over the impressively muscled arms of the guy talking to me. He could probably pick me up with one hand. "He's bigger than you are," I said, "but it's all about incentive. I told your friend he was getting extra shrimp, and I keep my word."

Amusement danced across his face.

The guy with the tacos was examining them. "I think I have to start counting the shrimp from now on so I know how many firstborns you're giving away."

"Uh oh..." I bit my lip in exaggerated guilt.

"Don't worry," the last guy chimed in, "he eats way too fast to count anything."

"All right. You guys are all set for now?"

They nodded at me as I hurried away to get the sandwich for James.

"Hello. I arrive with good news and bad news. Here's the good." I placed a plate in front of James. "The bad news is that Maggie has to go back to work now."

"Oh." Maggie pouted slightly as she jumped up.

"Thanks, Maggie," James said. "Maggie, thanks for sitting with me."

"Anytime." She grinned and dashed off.

The place began to fill up as it was nearly noon and I didn't get to talk to Maggie until it quieted down again after lunch. I found her in the kitchen, not doing anything but not looking bored.

"I hope you're not hating me for putting you with that guy who got stood up."

"No way." Maggie lit up as she showed me her teeth. "He was so funny. He kept saying I made his day."

"Maybe you did."

"All I did was keep him company for a few minutes."

"That was a nice thing to do and I think *I* owe you for it." I reached over to help myself to a drink.

"Heidi?" Maggie looked hesitant.

"Are you trying to collect already?" I teased her.

She shook her head but said, "Maybe."

"Well?"

"Okay, so I think I told you that I go to a bible study at my church on Wednesday nights when I don't have to work and this week we're all supposed to try to bring a friend and I looked at the schedule and saw that you get off at seven and since it starts at 7:30..." She lifted her red eyebrows in anticipation.

She'd laid out enough breadcrumbs for me to figure out where she was going with the question that didn't have a question. "Sure. I'll go."

"Awesome! It's my turn to bring the snacks so I'll bring something good."

"Do I need to bring anything?"

"Just your bible."

My bible? Why did that thought worry me? "Should I read something to prepare?"

"No, we'll read together. It's real informal." She mentioned looking forward to the bible study a few more times before the end of the shift and I started to feel like she was bringing me to school for show-and-tell.

~~~~

Maggie worked without me on Tuesday and I stayed home with the TV on all day. I kept it on constantly when I first moved out of my parents' house. I didn't watch it or even pay much attention to it. The low mumble was only something to simulate the background noise of a big family. I gradually weaned myself off it and got used to the quiet.

That Tuesday was different. And Wednesday morning, too. I kept the volume on the TV loud enough that I was always listening to it, keeping original thoughts at bay. I let myself analyze products I didn't need in commercials I didn't like to prevent my mind from focusing on John. A picture of him waiting for me outside the church was always on the edge of my thoughts, and I was determined to keep it relegated to the sidelines.

I was even happy to discover Griffin was working with me. He was good for distraction, both his incessant comments and the slack he left me to pick up.

"I saw you refilling drinks at my table," he said.

I was entering an order. There must have been a sign over that computer that only he could see that said, "Hey, Griffin, this is where Heidi is forced to stand still for you to talk to her."

"Don't worry," I said. "I told them you sent me."

"I wasn't worried. I know you have my back. And that you'd like to wrap your arms around it."

"Too bad that would be inappropriate at work."

Griffin gave me a very smug smile. "See, I just meant a hug and you're so into me your mind went straight to *inappropriate*."

I couldn't help it. I let him see me crack a smile. Only for a second. Then I got back to work. He found me again as people were beginning to trickle in for dinner. He leaned his back against the wall and waited for me to glance up at him. "You have no self-control, Heidi. Look at you ogling me every chance you get."

"You make it too easy, standing right in front of me."

"If I ever left this place, there would be such a huge hole in your heart. Admit it."

I put my hand over my heart. "I can't admit it. The idea is too painful."

"We're off at the same time tonight," he said. "Just say the word and we can have pleasure instead of pain."

"What crummy luck. I already have plans for tonight."

He shook his head with mock sadness. "I *know* you don't really have plans, but you did say you like to torture yourself."

"I do have plans."

"Please." He rolled his eyes. "You are such a bad liar. That's why I never believed you when you used to insist you wanted me to leave you alone. Let's do something tonight."

"Griffin, even if I wanted to spend time with you, I really did promise Maggie I'd do something with her."

"Your loss." He stepped outside for a smoke, even though one of the cooks was trying to flag him down for an order. I picked it up for him. He caught me one more time as I was leaving for the day and told me it was my last chance to have some fun with him. I continued to insist I already had plans and he continued to not believe me.

I hurried home after work and instead of simply putting on a clean shirt, I changed into one of my church dresses. It was a plain blue sundress. I expected the bible study to be fairly casual, but I preferred to be overdressed rather than underdressed when meeting new people. Especially since I wanted to make a good impression for Maggie's sake as well as my own.

That was where my bible was a concern. My parents gave it to me when I graduated from high school. There was hardly a wrinkle on the cover. Shouldn't a bible look more worn after eight years? Maybe no one would notice. Maybe they'd think it was new.

I knew it didn't matter. I already noticed and that was what was bugging me. I'd only recently admitted that my spiritual life had become lazy. That caused me to spend a day in prayer. And I broke up with someone because of it. Maybe I was allowed to be afraid to keep trying. Not that I was asking anyone's permission.

11

Maggie's church was across town from Sacred Heart, which actually made it fairly close to my apartment. It was a plain tan building with a wooden cross in front to identify it as a church. Maggie was waiting for me in the parking lot. She was wearing jeans and I was used to seeing her with her hair tied back so she looked a little different with the red curls around her face, younger maybe.

"Hi, Maggie."

She greeted me with a sound that wasn't exactly hi. It started with hi but ended with a squeal. "I'm so glad you came. I was already inside to put out the snacks – I brought pretzels with dip and cookies – and only two other people brought friends."

"Am I late?"

She checked the time on her phone and said, "You're perfect," then waved at me to follow her into the building. We entered through glass doors at the back of a sanctuary and turned immediately down a short hallway. We passed a room full of toys and entered a small classroom. There was a blank whiteboard on one wall and a table of snacks and drinks opposite. A few people were at that table and a few were seated in the circle of chairs in the middle of the room.

A skinny man with a skinny ring of hair around his head rushed up as we walked in. "Welcome, Maggie," he said. "Who did you bring with you?"

"This is my friend, Heidi Ray."

The man put his hand out to me. "Pastor Rob. Why don't you ladies help yourselves to some refreshments and then we'll get started."

I'd barely shaken his hand before Maggie nudged me towards the food. I filled a cup and put a few cookies on a plate while she gave me a verbal tour of the room. "Pastor Rob's been here about three years, but I've only been coming to his bible study for one. That's Cindy over there and Shannon. And Tiffany is the one they're both listening to. Tiffany's nice, but she talks a *lot*. Sometimes we all have to remind her to let someone else have a turn. See the two guys... the one on the right is Ryan. Don't talk to him unless you have to. He's asked out everyone in the group except me."

"Do you—"

She cut me off with narrowed eyes. "That's not the point."

"Okay. Who's the other guy?"

"Him I don't know," she said. "He came with Ryan. And I don't know the girl sitting down in the middle there. She must have come with either Kara, with the flowery shirt, or Claire, who's in red. Claire is super smart. Whenever someone is trying to remember where something is in the bible, she'll flip to it like it was bookmarked. Usually even before Rob."

The pastor urged everyone to gather around as Maggie mentioned him. "Small group today," he observed, "even with friends. Why don't we start by introducing the newcomers?"

Maggie popped out of her chair before his eyes fully landed on her. "This is Heidi," she said, her fingers waving at me like long distance tickles. "She works with me and she is so wonderful. She trained me and was the best teacher ever. If you go to The Sleepy Crab and ask for Heidi, you'll have maybe the best meal ever."

She sat down. It was a good thing I usually loved Maggie because that might have been the most embarrassing introduction ever. The two other friends were introduced more succinctly. Rob led a short prayer before he instructed us to open to James. Maggie was right about it being informal. He asked someone to read a few verses then opened the room to comments or questions. He pointed to another passage when the discussion died out, which was the moment Tiffany put her hand over her own mouth. A few others laughed kindly.

As soon as the word temptation came up, the discussion turned pretty light with several jokes about what favorite foods did to people's willpower. We got more serious as prayer became the topic. I mostly listened but made a few comments when I felt comfortable. Then Rob posed a question that pulled my comfort zone right out from under me. In fact, I think he threw it out the window.

"Can anyone talk about a time when you were afraid to pray, perhaps because you didn't want or didn't think you'd like the answer?"

"How can anyone be afraid to pray?" Maggie asked.

"I was," Tiffany said. "My grandmother battled cancer many years ago and the whole family was praying for her and asking their friends to pray for her and I... I didn't want to because I thought if she died, I'd be mad at God. Eventually I realized that if she died and I hadn't prayed I'd be mad at myself." She gave a tiny shrug. "Given that choice, prayer seemed obvious. God's a lot stronger than I am. I figured he could take the anger better. My grandmother actually beat the cancer and died a few years later from a heart problem. I was more equipped to deal with it because I'd already faced the possibility of her passing before and knew God was going to be there even if I didn't get the answer I wanted. I suppose it has as much to do with natural maturity – I was only a teenager when the cancer hit – but we all go through experiences as we grow to test or strengthen our faith. I can't say I won't run into a problem that affects me or my prayer life even more years from now."

"Thanks, Tiffany," Rob jumped in as she paused to take a breath. "It looked like Cindy had something to say."

Cindy nodded. "I'm dealing with something now that... I'm not sure it's fear exactly but... I think I've told you all that I was adopted as a baby. I've been thinking a lot lately about trying to find my birth parents. But I haven't prayed about it because I feel like there are too many questions. Should I tell my parents first? How do I tell them? What if my birth mother doesn't want to be found? What if... Anyway, I guess it isn't answers I'm afraid of, but that I might not interpret them correctly."

I saw heads nodding around me. I understood, too. But what I understood was incredibly humbling. I felt like the smallest person in the room and didn't contribute anything else the rest of the time. I simply listened and tried to learn and waited for it to be over.

Maggie noticed I had gotten quiet. I could tell by the questioning glances she sent my way. She waited until we had walked out to her car together to ask me if something was wrong.

"I kind of wish I hadn't come here tonight."

"Oh." Her shoulders collapsed and I kicked myself hard for making her feel bad.

"No, no," I said quickly. "Maggie, I said that wrong. I'm happy you invited me. This was a good group and I'd come again if you wanted me to, I just... I'm really stuck on that bit about being afraid to pray."

"Stuck? What do you mean?"

"I'm stuck. I just keep playing it over and over in my head. They were talking about facing death and major life upheaval. They had real problems and you know what mine is... the big crisis I'm afraid to take to God?"

Maggie slowly shook her head.

"My problem is that I think... I think I love someone."

"Uh..." She looked like she wanted to laugh but could see how serious I was. Her forehead creased. "You love everyone, Heidi. That's what makes you awesome."

"No. I mean I might be *in love* with someone. I'm worried about a guy problem."

Understanding and concern covered Maggie's face. "I thought you were handling the breakup well. Have you heard from Tyler? Did he ask you to reconsider or something?"

"No, it's not Tyler." I pinched my lips together before I let the truth out. My face was so hot I was sure the words would appear in a puff of steam. "I'm talking about John. John Myrie."

"John as in Tyler's best friend John?" The surprise made her face jerk as though she really had been hit with a blast of heat. "Whoa!"

"That John," I said.

"But I thought..." Maggie looked confused. Probably because I'd repeatedly told her how I could hardly stand to have

John around because he barely covered his negative thoughts about me.

"I've been wrong about a lot of things."

"Wow." She tipped her head hesitantly. "How do you know you were wrong?"

"He's been trying to be nice since the breakup. I think he feels bad about seeing it coming. I think that's why I thought he didn't like me, just that he saw a future where Tyler and I were unhappy and he couldn't say anything about it."

"Oh," Maggie said with a nod. "That would be a hard position."

"But now I'm so confused I want him to leave me alone entirely. I almost wish I still believed he hated me."

"Why?" Maggie squinted at me. "I mean, if you like him..."

"Because... just because maybe he doesn't hate me doesn't mean he has any interest in dating me. In fact, I know he doesn't because..." It was too embarrassing to admit he'd given away my phone number when I offered it. I shook off that thought. "And even if he did, he probably couldn't say anything because of Tyler and mostly I want him to stay away because being around him makes me feel so guilty I can hardly stand it."

"Guilty?"

"I've known John a long time. If I'm feeling something for him, it didn't just happen since I broke up with Tyler. I am not *allowed* to like him."

"Oh." Maggie stretched out the word while she tried to nod and shake her head at the same time. "I see," she said, her voice nearly an octave higher than normal. "And I have no advice for you whatsoever."

Her helpless admission put a smile on my face. It made me feel as though my emotional struggle was not completely insignificant after all. I wasn't exactly happy about that, but I was happy someone listened to it.

"But I will pray for you and maybe that will make it easier for you to get started."

"Thanks, Maggie. I'll see you at work tomorrow."

I knew before we went our separate ways – I knew before I even talked to Maggie – that I had decided to stop running from myself. I wasn't putting it off anymore. I was waiting for the right time. I got into my pajamas as soon as I got home, even though it was earlier than usual. I lay in my bed and closed my eyes to distractions. Then I opened my heart to examination.

It wasn't difficult to figure out what I was feeling. The hard part was facing it all. I'd been telling myself for a long time that John's disapproval bothered me so much because I felt bad for Tyler being stuck in the middle. I'd been lying to myself. I cared a great deal for John. I couldn't say I was fully in love with him because I'd mostly done a good job stunting my feelings while I was with Tyler. But even while I refused to acknowledge or identify those romantic flutters for John, they'd still been there. Did that make me guilty of betrayal? Or how guilty was I?

I took a deep breath and began to pray out loud, because it had helped before and because my biggest worry was going to eat me up if I didn't let it out. "God... did I use Tyler? Did I stay with him longer than I should have because I didn't want to stop seeing John through him? It didn't occur to me until I saw John waiting outside the church. I was so relieved, so relieved that I might still..." I put my hands on my face and tried to listen quietly to find the answer in myself.

I prayed until I began to let go of some shameful feelings. I had done the best I could. If I'd stayed with Tyler for the wrong reasons, I hadn't done it intentionally. I truly believed I hadn't. All I could do now was be honest with myself – and everyone else – going forward. I promised God that if I ever again agreed to get married, I would be able to say a slow and deliberate yes. Not just okay.

I felt my body finally relaxing and could almost hear God agreeing with my contemplation on the exhale. *You'll be okay, Heidi.* I would. Once the guilt was stripped away, the situation was pretty simple. I was infatuated with a guy who didn't feel the same way about me. Countless others had survived that and I would, too. I smiled to myself as I thought about what John would think of me deciding to be okay.

12

I worked the later shift on Thursday, and it took me a minute to put my finger on what was different about the restaurant. It was quiet since people hadn't started filling the place up for dinner yet. I tied on an apron and walked into the kitchen. That's when I realized that the music was a classic rock ballad that had nothing to do with pirate ships or buried treasure.

"Hi, Heidi." Maggie was chatting with one of the cooks.

"No pirate music today?" I asked.

"And probably never again," she said with a grin. "Griffin quit."

The cook she was talking to turned and fist-bumped the guy next to him. I wondered only briefly at their delight being possibly overdone. Griffin was lazy, but cooks didn't make up for that and surely he never accused the guys of undressing him with their eyes.

My thoughts were interrupted by another server returning to the kitchen with an appetizer that was a mistake. Several of us grabbed a bite of that delicious mistake.

Maggie helped me with a big crowd before she went home for the day. A young couple came in making moony eyes at each other. They were very cute and it made me think of John before I pushed the thought away. Just because maybe he didn't hate me didn't mean I had any chance with him. I couldn't completely squelch the hope that he might change his mind about me, but I shouldn't let my thoughts dwell where I might get hurt. I had decided that I would make sure I said hello if I saw him at coffee and donuts on Sunday. Hello was where we needed to be and where I needed to accept we would likely stay.

I had just taken drink orders from that young couple when the man chased me down. "Hey. Heidi, right? Can you help me?"

"I'll try. What do you need?"

"I... uh..." He glanced back at his table, presumably to make sure the girl wasn't looking. "I'm going to propose tonight."

The Sleepy Crab was great, but it wasn't terribly romantic so I'd only gotten to help with one other proposal before. I dropped a ring in a glass that time. Bringing it to the table had been thrilling. My cheeks ached with the force of the smile this man had prompted. "What do you want me to do?" I asked.

"Can you bring this out with the food?" He took a pretty ring from his pocket and held it up. There was no box. "Don't put it *in* the food because I think she'd hate that, but somewhere like on the side of the plate so she'll see it right away."

I nodded and took the ring. "I'll do my best."

"Great." He started to turn away then met my eyes seriously. "Please don't lose that. It was my grandmother's."

"I got it," I assured him. He made me nervous though and I carefully checked my pocket for holes before I dropped the ring into it for later. It was difficult to look as though I knew nothing when I brought the drinks, but I don't think the woman suspected anything.

I greeted a group of teenage girls next. "Welcome to The Sleepy Crab, ladies."

"What happened to the music?" one of them asked.

"You liked the pirate music?"

"Not exactly," she said. "But I brought my friends just so they could hear how bad it was."

"Sorry to disappoint you. That was... temporary."

The girl who asked sat back with a puzzled frown, sort of like she wasn't sure if she was disappointed or not.

The friend next to her said, "We're just here for dessert. Is that okay?"

"Absolutely. If you ate dinner first you wouldn't have room for dessert, and they're all really good."

She smiled and the posture of a few girls relaxed as well. They seemed to be afraid of offending me by not running up a bill. If only they knew how well I understood and endorsed that concept of frugality. "Do you want to go ahead and order with drinks or do you need a minute to narrow down the choices?"

"Um… well, I think we're all going to have water and…" She looked at her friends and though they had nodded at the mention of water, they now looked uncertain.

"No problem," I said. "I'll grab five waters while you all talk over dessert."

I passed Michelle before I got back to their table. "Heidi," she said, "do you think you could come in tomorrow? Madeline just called in sick, and I'm already down Griffin."

"Yeah." I nodded happily. I could always use the hours. "I guess Griffin didn't give you much notice?"

She shook her head. "Just told me yesterday when he came in that it'd be his last shift."

We all expected Griffin to quit at any time, but something about the departure bothered me. I think it was because he hadn't told me. He'd talked to me several times and hadn't told *me* it was his last shift. "Well, you know, I've already had one request to put the pirate music back on."

"Ack. No." She rolled her eyes in disgust. "We put up with that too long as it is. Griffin told me he'd have quit weeks ago if I hadn't made it a challenge." She brushed by me in a hurry. I was left with a funny feeling in my stomach. A queasy icky funny feeling in my stomach.

Griffin knew? He knew the pirate music was intended to annoy him into quitting? My mind flashed to the cooks fist-bumping each other over his departure and the cheer another server had let out when someone told her. He'd been an outsider from the beginning, given the job at the request of the owners. We'd never given him a chance to earn a place, had we? I had joked to Maggie that Griffin's attitude might be some sort of armor, and I was suddenly sure of it. How would I act if I knew everyone was waiting to throw a party when I left?

If I had started kidding back sooner, would he have let his guard down? At least enough to tell me he was leaving without assuming I would join in the celebration? I'd never know. And he would never know that he had in fact poked a tiny hole in my heart. I would pray for him. Now that I was getting my prayer life back in order, Griffin would stay in my thoughts whether he knew it or not.

I collected those thoughts for later and delivered the drinks I was carrying. "So what kind of sweets are we having tonight, ladies?"

The girls tossed around some indecisive looks. One of them finally turned to me. "Sorry. We're having some rough negotiations here. We're trying to figure out who should order what so we can share and…"

"… and nobody else wants Key lime pie." The girl who finished the thought gave her friends a playful glare. "What is wrong with you people that no one else likes Key lime pie? I can't eat a whole one *and* sample something else."

"Maybe I can help." I'd worked there long enough that Michelle gave me a lot of leeway on special orders. This seemed like an excellent time to take advantage. "I'm not very busy right now so I have time to get creative. If you each tell me two or three things you want, I can cut up the desserts in the kitchen and bring them out as sampler plates."

"Really?" Two of the girls spoke at once, and they all looked excited. There was no way I couldn't do it now.

"Sure. Let's see what this looks like and I'll figure out a fair way to charge you. I promise it won't be any more than if you each order an individual dessert."

"Wow. Thanks."

I got my notepad ready and they began making choices. It didn't come out nearly as complicated as it might have. That lone request for Key lime pie was the only problem. Everything else got split three to five ways. I hadn't had any dessert myself so I had a pretty good idea how to solve the problem of the extra pie.

The girls thanked me again and again when I brought desserts out and by the time I got back to the kitchen, the order was ready for that ring in my pocket. The woman at that table, unfortunately, had requested a messy salad that covered the whole plate. Anywhere along the edge that I tried to place the ring, it would slide right into the greens. I tried to hook the stone over the outside edge, but that looked precarious. I was *not* going to lose the ring and dropping it on the floor next to the woman was not the most romantic way to deliver it either.

I picked up a small saucer and set the ring on it. It sort of wobbled and slid off-center as I picked up the plate. It just didn't feel like a good presentation. I looked around the kitchen. A napkin! I put it gently over the ring, thinking I could unveil it at the table. That didn't feel right either. He'd said he wanted her to see it right away, and I didn't like it being out of my sight when I kept hearing him beg me not to lose it.

As I picked up the napkin again, a better idea hit me. I rolled it up and slipped it through the ring. Then I set it on the plate with the stone facing up. That worked. That worked perfectly. I hoped. I felt excited for the woman who was a complete stranger, more so than I had when...

I took the long way around so I could approach from the woman's back. I stopped at my table of teenage girls and asked how the treats were working out.

"Awesome."

"Perfect."

"You're the best."

This was a wonderful night to be at work. I leaned closer to the table and whispered to them, "I'm about to present an engagement ring if you girls want to see something cool."

All five of them made the same exact hushed shriek. I felt their eyes on me as I approached the couple. I walked up slowly, trying to catch the man's eye so he could wave me off if he wasn't ready.

When he saw me, he sat back and said, "Looks like the food's here," rather loudly. He sounded nervous but was, apparently, ready.

I set his food down first so I'd be able to get out of the way as soon as the ring was on the table. "And for you, ma'am, a Waking Crab Salad. It comes with a special side today."

She gasped as I put the small plate with the ring in front of her. Then I took several steps back to give them some privacy. He talked for a minute – lowly – and I was glad I couldn't hear. Then he got down on his knee next to her. I had backed up enough that I was next to the teenagers again. The man returned to his seat as I suddenly wished I could hear just one of the words I didn't hear.

"What did she say?" one of the girls hissed from behind me. That's what I wanted to know.

I turned to shrug at them. "Don't worry though. I can find out."

They waved me away to work on that.

I stopped in the kitchen for a bite of pie and to give the couple time to taste their food. Then I made another round through the dining room. "How did everything come out over here?" I looked between them. Between their smiles and the ring being on the woman's hand, I had a guess.

"It's very good." The somewhat clueless man nodded at his plate. He thought I wanted to know about the food.

His fiancée smiled bigger and waved her ring-clad finger at me.

"Excellent," I said. "Let me know if you need anything."

I walked by the girls with my thumb up and they all giggled happily. Those girls ended up staying until we closed. They were the last to leave. We didn't need the table, and I enjoyed having some life in the place. Their table was easy to clear as I'd taken all the plates a while before they left. The other servers had gone home, and it was strange that Michelle wasn't in the lobby to lock up. I went to the office to let her know the dining room was empty.

She was at her desk, dabbing her eyes with a tissue.

"Michelle?"

She looked up. "Do you need something?"

"Just wanted to tell you it's clear up front. Is something wrong?"

"I just... I've never felt so childish."

"About?" Surely it wasn't childish to cry if something was wrong.

She put her elbow on the desk and propped her chin on her hand to look up at me. "He told me from day one that he didn't want to be here, that he only took the job because his grandparents insisted. I convinced myself the music was... it seemed a harmless way to give him an excuse to quit but now... she sounded so scared."

I watched Michelle bury her face in her hands as though I was standing a mile away and not a few feet. The moment seemed impossible and too real at the same time. Something was wrong. And something was wrong with me that I didn't want to know what it was. I asked anyway. "Michelle?"

"I just got off the phone with Barb Dewitt."

That was the woman I knew as *Mrs.* Dewitt. I also knew her as Griffin's grandmother, and I thought that might be more important at the moment.

"Griffin didn't come home last night," Michelle said. "She said he rarely even goes out anymore except for work, and he's never not come home. She's really worried. She's been calling people all day and hasn't found anyone who's seen him since he left here yesterday."

Since he asked me to do something with him. Since he told me it was my last chance to do something with him.

"She wanted to know if he'd called in sick for tomorrow. She didn't know he quit."

What else didn't he tell anyone?

Michelle had trained her eyes on the flat carpet. Her head moved slowly side to side. "I have a really bad feeling. What kind of a manager am I that I try to drive someone away rather than help him be better? What kind of a *person* am I that I treat a kid..."

I tried to laugh at Michelle calling Griffin a kid. He was younger than me, but I wasn't so old he seemed like a kid. She had two daughters about his age though. One was twenty as well and one was two years older. If I remembered right. I was trying to call to mind all the times she'd told me her kids' ages to calculate how old they were now because numbers were detached and unemotional and safe even while my conscience was whispering to me that people didn't disappear for no reason.

"Maybe he's... He's not the most considerate person. Maybe he's just busy with something and not realizing he's worrying his grandparents." I didn't believe that. My voice didn't believe that. Michelle didn't believe it either. My instinct was to say something to try to make her feel better.

She nodded at the attempt. "Do you want me to let you know if I hear anything?"

"Yes. Actually, can you give me his number? And his grandmother's? Is she… Do you think she'd mind if I called her?"

"Oh, no. She's real nice. I'm sure she'd be glad to know you're concerned." Michelle read Mrs. Dewitt's number from her phone and then began rummaging through a desk drawer. She always struck me as organized in her head even when her office wasn't. "Here it is." She read Griffin's number to me as well. I thanked her and said goodnight.

It was nearly 10 PM when I got home and I wrestled with myself about whether or not it was too late to call a woman I hardly knew. Griffin had still been missing an hour ago. There was no way she was sleeping. I dialed with bated breath and told her who I was as I tried to let it out. She said there'd been no news and thanked me for my concern. I couldn't believe it had been any good for her, but I was on the list of people to call when he showed up now.

I stared at Griffin's name on my phone. I was praying for him. It didn't matter to me if he knew that, but if there was any chance it would matter to him, I should tell him. But what could I say? I couldn't pretend this suddenly made us good friends. I considered what I was to Griffin – a now former coworker who was fun to annoy – and tried to compose a thought that would show concern on that level. A disturbing image of someone in a police uniform reading the message instead stilled my fingers for a moment. I dismissed that image with a decision not to entertain the possibility of a sad ending.

I'm going to sleep now so I can dream about you being safe in bed.

Satisfied, I hit send. That said I wanted him to be safe, but using the word bed would allow Griffin to twist it into something that would amuse him. Then I called my parents. It wasn't as late where they were. Mom listened to what was going on in my life. She heard that I was more worried about Griffin than I let on and less conflicted about John than I said. And I knew how much it meant to her to have an adult child who still needed her to hear those things.

Dad was proud of my attempt to keep the washing machine running on my own. He encouraged me to call him next time I tackled even a minor repair so he could brag to his buddies. That was going to be so embarrassing if I bumped into any of those buddies who still lived in Thompsonville.

I noticed a new text as I hung up and almost dropped the phone before I realized it was from Tyler. `Tigers lost today and Myrie won't cook for just me.`

Possible subtext in his message swirled with my already frazzled emotions. Was Tyler missing me the same way I was missing him? Was it simply hard to change the routines that had included each other or was there a hint of regret? Surely he was only being friendly. He'd said he hoped we could be friendly and ignoring him would not be. I replied: `Sorry about all that. Should I send you some easy recipes?`

Tyler: `Your condolences are enough.`

13

Contrary to the flurry of contacts that night, my phone sat bleakly inactive when I returned to it the next morning. No news, good or bad, had reached me. No change in my mental state either. I didn't feel the fresh start that a good night's sleep usually brings. It was as though I had simply gone into my bedroom and walked out again after a few seconds and not nine hours.

I went through the motions of taking care of myself. Breakfast. Shower. Battle with the dying but still perfectly good hairdryer. I wore my favorite black pants that only looked faded when I held them against the newest pair.

I entered The Sleepy Crab a few minutes before we opened for lunch and right behind another server named Peter. He'd worked with me about three years and was either thirty-seven or thirty-eight. He had a birthday the first week of June and insisted he was turning thirty-seven. I would have sworn he was already thirty-seven but didn't know why anyone would lie about an age in the middle of a decade. He held the door for me. "Morning, Heidi."

"Hey, Peter. How are you today?"

"Good, you?" He picked up two clean aprons and held one out to me.

I mumbled something in response to his question and took the apron. "Thanks."

He watched me tie the strings. "You okay? I don't want to pry, but you don't look like yourself."

"Who do I look like?"

He smiled. "That's more like it. I thought you were dragging there for a minute but must have been projecting the fact that *I* didn't want to get out of bed this morning." The speakers kicked on and Peter looked up at the nearest one as though he could see the music coming out of it. "Bon Jovi?" he asked. "Does that mean what I think it means?"

"Michelle's done with the pirate songs."

His eyebrows stayed up in question. "But does that mean Griffin's gone?"

"He quit," I said.

"Good riddance." Peter continued to mutter under his breath as he moved into the kitchen, something about a disgusting plan for Griffin's food if he ever showed his face for a meal.

I knew Griffin had brought most of the derision on himself, but I still hated to hear it. Not because he was missing. Because I hated to remember how I had indulged in it myself not too long ago. I had laughed when coworkers joked about running him down in the parking lot or locking him in the cooler. For a while, we'd all made a game of seeing who got the rudest comment from him in a given day. But no matter how hard Griffin was to be around, continuing to talk about him after he'd left said as much about the rest of us as it did about him.

I walked up front rather than follow Peter to the kitchen where I normally waited for customers. Michelle was talking to a fairly new hostess and stepped away when she saw me coming. She waved me into a corner and whispered, "Have you heard anything?"

I shook my head. "You?"

"No. I haven't told anyone else here. Do you think we should?"

I shook my head again. "Given the general opinion he left, I think we'd be generating more gossip than concern."

"You're probably right. Thanks for coming in today, by the way."

"No problem."

Michelle blew out a heavy breath as she headed back to her office. She rarely took a full day off, though she slipped in and out during quiet times when she needed to tend to something going on in her life. The insane hours had never seemed to take a toll before, but she walked away just then like someone carrying a significant weight.

I paced the dining room for a few minutes, alternating my thoughts between worrying about Griffin and feeling like a self-centered adolescent for worrying about Tyler's text as well. Was he taking the breakup harder than I thought? Would I see him or John on Sunday? I was trying to brace myself for an empty bench outside the church or one with Tyler on it. At the same time, I wondered how any of that could seem important when I might be on the verge of hearing about some horrible tragedy.

The hostess caught my eye as she led a small group to my section. I took a calming breath, said a quick prayer, and banished all non-work thoughts from my mind. Time to channel Heidi Ray, the dedicated server Maggie looked up to.

"Hi, ladies. I'm Heidi and I'll be taking excellent care of you today. Have you been to The Sleepy Crab before?"

Three women of varying ages looked up at me and slowly shook their heads as though I might yell at them for being new.

"Welcome. I'm delighted you decided to give us a try. Please let me know if you have any questions. Can I start you with something to drink?"

"Diet Coke."

"Diet Coke."

"Iced tea."

"I'll give you a minute to look over the menu while I grab those."

They weren't so much looking over the menu as they were scrutinizing it when I returned. One woman had the pointer finger of each hand pinning the pages to the table while her eyes darted between the two marked locations. The other two women were having a discussion about cheese that might have been helping them choose what to eat and might have been related to something far more philosophical.

"The longer it's aged, the more... flavor it takes on," one was saying as I set the iced tea in front of her.

"But the sharper taste can be overpowering. There's no balance."

"Here you are," I said as I set a drink in front of the last woman. "Shall I give you a few more minutes to decide?"

The woman with her fingers on the menu looked up long enough to say, "Please."

I nodded and moved on to some new arrivals. "Welcome. You all are early today."

A few of them smiled at me. A man with a deep voice I happened to know sounded authentic saying "Arr, Matey," said, "We're just so happy it's Friday. Thought if we had lunch early, we could trick the boss into letting us go home early."

"Good plan," I said. "Let's pretend I need you to tell me what you want to drink today so anyone who wants a change has a chance to speak up." I gestured to the person on my left to start and followed the voices around the table.

"Water."

"Diet Coke."

"Diet Coke."

"Coke."

"Thin Cola."

"Water."

"Diet Coke."

I wrote everything down, then backed up to narrow my eyes at Mr. Wildcard. "Thin Cola?"

"That's an easy one," he said. "You don't remember it?"

"Sorry."

"Half Coke, half Sprite."

"Okay. That does sound familiar. Back with these drinks in two shakes of a lamb's tail."

He snickered and said, "Speaking of familiar," as I walked away. Guess I'd used that line on them a few times.

My feet halted two steps into the kitchen as people seemed to be standing in unusual places and someone was yelling, "For pity's sake, go to the sink!" over incoherent grumbling. A survey of the commotion told me that one of the cooks had cut himself. And that the work station that now needed to be sanitized was getting a lot more sympathy.

"*Why* would you just stand there bleeding all over the place?"

"Didn't anyone ever tell you knives are sharp?"

The guy was rinsing his wound, and it didn't look serious. I resumed my mission to collect drinks. I put in the order for my larger group before those first three women made their decisions. Then I was on my way to drop off a few refills when a familiar voice said, "Hi, Heidi."

I stopped alongside one of Peter's tables and saw Tyler and John. They already had food so I'd apparently walked past them several times without noticing. It wasn't strange that they hadn't asked for me. Tyler never did. He said it might make me look unprofessional. But it still *felt* strange, though not nearly as awkward as I expected.

"Hi," I said, looking at Tyler only because he was the one who had stopped me and because John was staring at his plate as though he was trying to be invisible. "You guys having a good week?"

Tyler tipped his head thoughtfully. "Could be worse. How are things here?"

"Not bad. Maggie still thinks I'm awesome."

"You must be feeling some relief… based on what's coming out of the speakers. Or not coming out." He indicated one of those speakers with a jerk of his head.

"Oh, um…" I wanted to confide that I wasn't relieved, that I'd gladly trade cheesy music and vulgar remarks for the heavy anxiety that something bad had happened. But I couldn't. It wouldn't be the time or place for a serious talk even if I didn't have a big ex label on me now. "I guess," I said. "I should…" I nodded towards the tray in my hand. "These drinks aren't for you so I need to…"

"Of course," Tyler said. "Good to see you, Heidi."

"Same here," John said.

I smiled at both of them as I walked away. Part of my brain was still thinking about John as I set the glasses in front of their recipients. He'd smiled at his plate when I said Maggie still thought I was awesome. I'd let myself believe he was amused by my quip and not just me. That was a welcome change.

I was entering an order into the computer a short time later when my phone buzzed in my pocket. I rushed through the last few buttons and slid the phone out enough to see who was calling. Mrs. Dewitt.

I pushed against the side door as I answered, glad that no one else was taking an outside break at the moment. "Hi, Mrs. Dewitt," I said. "This is Heidi Ray." My voice quavered just a bit, distracted by my brain chanting *good news, good news, good news.*

"Glad I caught you, Heidi. I wanted to let you know that Griffin finally came home safe and sound early this morning."

There was a pause while I waited for more. I wanted to know what happened. I wanted to know where he'd been. I wanted to know why no one called me sooner. There were other questions flooding my head, too. All of them nosy and/or impertinent. I settled for a leading statement. "I really appreciate you giving me an update."

"We talked with Griffin for a long time, asking him where he was, trying to make it clear how much he'd scared me and his grandfather. He... And I'd like to ask you a favor," she said crisply.

"Um... okay?"

Her hesitation was palpable through the phone. "I trust you can be discreet."

"Of course." I meant it, but my assurance came out as a reflex, pushed out by curiosity. My fingers began to drum nervously against the back of the phone.

"We did most of the talking this morning. Griffin wouldn't say much. At one point though, he said we didn't need to worry because he didn't have the guts to go through with it and I'm so afraid he meant to harm himself." Her voice became overly crisp and began to crack. "We've lined up a therapist and Griffin refuses to go. Says he'll be fine now. I... Will you talk to him and get him to go for us?"

My first instinct was no. My relationship with Griffin consisted of a few weeks of jokey innuendo. How could I talk to him about something so serious? But there was so much anguish in his grandmother's voice. A refusal sounded incredibly harsh even in my head. "Isn't there... I'm sure there's someone he'd listen to more than me."

"I know you two aren't close because he looked surprised when I mentioned you'd called me about him, but... He's pushed away all his high school friends these last few years and the only young man he sees much is... *Men* just don't know how to talk and I thought... sometimes it's actually easier to talk to someone not so close. I don't know who else to ask. Please. Will you try?"

~ 115 ~

It was even harder to say no when she was only asking me to try. "I doubt he'd... I can *try* to talk to him though."

"Thank you, dear. He's a good kid. I don't... I need to go."

It sounded as though she wanted to hang up because she was losing what was left of her composure. I stood outside for a moment and collected my own. I didn't have a clue how or when I could talk to Griffin. He hadn't replied to my text. But he was home right now and I was at work. I planned to finish my shift, which I'd barely started, and rack my brain for something to say to Griffin sometime in the evening.

New customers had just been seated when I got inside. I focused on serving lunch. It was a busy Friday afternoon and the time disappeared faster than our shrimp tacos. The middle of the day was a little quieter. Between customers, I helped Michelle stick tiny flags in the flowers on the tables in honor of the upcoming Independence Day. She seemed to have gotten over her relief that Griffin was okay and was muttering about how irresponsible it was for him to make everyone worry. I asked her where we should put the extra flags.

A cute family arrived for an early dinner while I was trying to figure out how to tie a flag to a string so that it would hang right-side-up. "How about table nine?" the hostess whispered to me, eyeing the flag as though she wanted to take over. I gladly traded jobs and led the family to one of my tables.

The mom was holding a baby that couldn't have been more than a month old. Only a tiny wrinkly face stuck out of the pink blanket. The dad ushered a boy who might have been three or four into the booth next to him. The boy was a small copy of his dad, right down to the matching black curls hanging down in the middle of their foreheads. When I asked what he wanted to drink, the little boy's lips moved but no sound came out.

"Chocolate milk?" I guessed.

He dipped his chin in what I interpreted as a nod even though it never came back up again. I went into the kitchen to pour the chocolate milk – and drinks for the kid's parents – and found Peter and the cook who had cut himself having a slow-motion sword fight. They had taken flags off a pair of short wooden sticks for their props. I tried not to roll my eyes at them. Perhaps Peter was a lot younger than thirty-seven.

Though the exaggerated – and also slow-motion – cheering they were getting amused me more than I wanted to admit.

I brought the drinks to the table still smiling over the ridiculous antics of my coworkers. Two more families were being seated. Those coworkers would be busy soon enough.

"Have you decided what you'd like to eat tonight?"

The parents gave me their orders then both of them looked at the young boy so I looked at him, too. He stared at me with wide eyes and a tightly closed mouth.

"Go on," his dad said, "tell her what you want."

The boy's eyes grew wider and his lips pressed together even tighter. It didn't appear as though either of his parents was going to order for him.

"Well," I said, "how about a meatball?"

His eyebrows scrunched slightly and he shook his head.

"You sure? I could have them make up a giant meatball, like as big as the table, and just plunk it right down here. That'd be a good dinner, right?"

He shook his head again and started to giggle.

"Okay. What sounds good to you then?"

The boy whispered, "Grilled cheese sandwich."

"Oh. That might be even better than a giant meatball. Do you want applesauce with it?"

He nodded at me and I assured all of them that their food would be ready soon. After I entered the order, I returned to the kitchen and pretended not to be disappointed that the sword fight was over.

My next customer got the shortest welcome I think I'd ever given. I said, "Hi," and then couldn't think of anything else. Eight years of "Welcome to The Sleepy Crab," "Thanks for visiting us today," and "I knew you couldn't stay away from the shrimp tacos," and I had nothing.

"I guess you didn't expect to see me twice in one day."

"Uh… I guess not." I'd prayed away the guilt of being attracted to John and I'd prayed away the grudge that clouded every interaction. He simply wasn't attracted to me. That wasn't anyone's fault. It wasn't fair, but it wasn't anyone's fault. Yet despite my progress on being okay, I stood there tongue-tied as though I still had a dozen or so problems where he was concerned.

"I felt like mac and cheese again," John said, calm as though we'd never had an uncomfortable relationship. "I've never found a recipe as good as what's here."

I inhaled slowly, feeling myself returning to my element. "If only you knew someone who worked here. Maybe she could get you some inside information."

"If only." John shook his head sadly in response to my sarcasm.

"Although if you didn't cut the recipe down a lot, you'd have your whole freezer full of macaroni."

"Oh, I could definitely live with that."

I laughed and pretended I needed to write down an order for one person. It was an excuse to look away. I didn't blush easily, but this was not a good time to push my luck. "You want water with that, or something else?"

"Water's fine."

"All right."

Words that looked like "two shakes of a lamb's tail" were on John's lips as I headed for the kitchen. We managed some pleasant banter each time I returned to his table. I put any thoughts of him having been sent by Tyler out of my head and relaxed, trying and mostly succeeding to pretend he was just like any other customer. Until he reminded me that he wasn't.

When I returned his card and wished him a good night, he said, "Heidi, you're off soon, right?"

I knew he was right, but I checked the time anyway. "Yeah. Should be slipping out of here in a few minutes."

"Can I wait for you?"

"Can you... wait?"

"I'd like to talk to you when you're done. If you don't mind me hanging around outside."

"No, I... that's fine."

I said it was fine. I wasn't sure that made it fine. I finished and clocked out with a weird nervous energy. It wasn't just John. I'd never been good with curiosity. I was the kind of kid who poked and shook not only my Christmas presents, but the ones with my siblings' names, too.

John was leaning against his car in the parking lot, which was right next to mine. His head was down so I thought he was looking at something on his phone. I didn't see him put anything away when he saw me though. He just stood a little straighter as I approached.

"Hey, Heidi."

"Hello again. I'm just running into you all day."

John offered me a meek smile. He knew that I knew that seeing him repeatedly where I worked was not exactly the coincidence I hinted it was. "You, uh… well, you looked upset about something at lunch, and I saw you duck out for a phone call that made you turn white. That's really why I came back. I wanted to ask if anything was wrong."

He'd come back here just to ask if anything was wrong? The only thing wrong at the moment was that I could now expect another round of remorse over the times I'd told my mom that the only problem with my relationship with Tyler was that his best friend was a horrible person. "No," I said. "The phone call this afternoon, that was actually good news. Sort of."

"Sort of? Is it not something you want to talk about?"

I wanted to tell him everything. Mrs. Dewitt had asked me to be discreet though. I'd told Michelle only that Griffin came home.

"Of course you don't have to. You don't need me to tell you that you don't have to tell me if you don't want to… tell me. Um… did that make sense?" John cocked his head to the side as he went over his wording.

The expression made my desire to tell him everything even stronger. I took a moment to reflect and decided that telling John wouldn't be gossiping. It would be sharing something on my mind with someone I trusted. I took an extra moment to solidify the thought that I trusted John. Then I told him how Griffin hadn't come home for two nights, what his grandmother suspected and what she'd asked of me. "How am I supposed to talk about something like that? With Griffin of all people?"

John was clearly surprised and he stared at me while he processed what I'd told him. "Making people comfortable is something you're good at," he said eventually. "You kind of do it for a living. Maybe it won't be as difficult as you think to talk to him."

"I know he won't listen."

"You'll feel better knowing you tried."

"Maybe."

"And he might listen. I don't know him so I could be wrong, but it's possible that all the innuendo was him – very badly – reaching out to you. Maybe he sensed your loving heart." John's hand had floated up while he talked and came within inches of touching my face before he snapped it back to his side.

There was tenderness in the gesture that I couldn't accept because I was too busy denying his words. A loving heart? Maggie had been offering me friendship for months while I'd taken her compliments and given nothing in return. I mistreated Tyler by dating him without appreciating what that could mean. And I still hadn't been in touch with my granddad about rescheduling my visit.

Then a whisper in the back of my mind suggested I was being too hard on myself. I'd been the most uncharitable to the man in front of me, and he'd apparently forgiven me. He'd forgiven me without an apology. Right there was an opportunity to prove I could do the loving thing. "I still hope Griffin's grandparents get him into therapy without my help, but I'll talk to him if I can. First I need to talk to you though. I need to say… I'm sorry. I… well, things were awkward between us and I know now that was mostly my fault. Or actually, it was completely my fault. I'm sorry for that."

"I'm not sure I'd say awkward."

"Difficult?"

"Yes." He closed his eyes for a moment, perhaps against memories of those difficult times. "But it wasn't your fault."

"It was," I insisted. "We both know it was. Not only did I run with the assumption that you were, you know, not my biggest fan, but I only let myself entertain prejudicial reasons for that. I was very unfair to you and I want you to know that now that I understand. I get that you were in a tight spot."

"Do you?"

"Yeah." I said it slowly, becoming uncertain as the word left my mouth. John looked as though he doubted we were on the same page.

"What do you understand?" he said.

"That it was hard for you to sit back and watch me and Tyler making a mistake."

"I admit I," John looked up as he searched for words, "that I thought he wasn't the best match for you. But I wasn't in a position to judge."

"I don't know. You saw us together more than anyone else and obviously you were right. We didn't fit. I'd say you were a good judge."

John shrugged uneasily and I didn't blame him. Right or not, it wasn't as though I was congratulating him on predicting a happy event.

If there was any chance Tyler wanted to try again, I thought I'd just done a good job closing that door. And he hadn't looked bothered to see me that afternoon. I wanted to test the waters for moving forward as friends. "Maybe it wouldn't be too weird for the three of us to get together again sometime, though probably not right away. Tyler might not mind if I came over to watch a game with you guys if I brought food. Don't you think?"

John appeared to consider the merits of the idea at the same time my feet began to remind me I'd been standing on them all day. Maybe we'd let the idea sink in. "Speaking of baseball," I said, "aren't you missing a game right now?"

"Tyler can catch me up."

"I should let you go so you're not too far behind."

John sort of nodded, but he didn't offer a farewell or make any move to indicate our conversation had come to an end.

I turned to leave as I said, "Goodnight."

"Heidi, wait."

I stopped and opened my mouth to ask why.

John burst out with, "I love you."

A sturdy dam sprang up around my heart to contain the emotions that threatened to spill over. Love had so many forms. Did John mean that he was willing to maintain a friendly relationship with me even if Tyler wasn't? Or did he...? Oh, wow. My brain was receiving a signal that my mouth was still open. I couldn't seem to find the controls to the muscle that would close it.

"Do you know that... that we flipped a coin?"

Who flipped a what!? Was he doing what he'd done outside the church, starting one conversation and then turning it into something else? I closed my mouth as I firmly set my jaw. My head began to shake, trying to indicate that it was absolutely not acceptable to change the subject after starting with *I love you*. I needed to know what he meant.

John shifted his weight nervously. I felt a twinge of satisfaction that my silence was affecting him.

"You look like you don't know what I'm talking about so I think you don't know that we – Tyler and I – we flipped a coin over who was going to call you."

He was going to try to stick with the new topic. My mind unwillingly began to sift through memories where one of them might have called me. There wasn't anything significant enough to be brought up. Not when there was an *I love you* hanging in the air between us.

"You still look confused," John said. "Maybe Tyler was right. Maybe you didn't realize..." He studied me for a few moments before he started talking fast. "I guess you've forgotten if you even knew you did it, but way back when you first wrote your number on Tyler's receipt, you set it down in front of me. Tyler was convinced you just mixed them up by mistake. I thought – and maybe it was wishful thinking – but I thought you'd done it on purpose to signal sort of an open mind because... well, you didn't know either of us that well and we'd both hinted..."

Oh, no. Oh, no no no. I was catching up and I wished I was still confused. I wrote my number on Tyler's receipt? I wrote my number on *Tyler's* receipt. I remembered how I'd scribbled it out quickly before any of my coworkers could see what I was doing and how I'd rushed away from the table before John or Tyler could say anything about the number. All this time I thought John had received a clear and unwanted message and I'd written my number on Tyler's receipt.

John wasn't asking me now whether he or Tyler had been right about my intentions and I didn't want to tell him – didn't think I *could* tell him – that we were all wrong. I most of all had been wrong. I put my fingers on my temple while John continued to explain.

"I know it was juvenile to flip a coin. It was my idea but I was half-kidding. Then I couldn't say that after I lost. Believe me when I say it was one moment of stupidity that I have lived to regret."

"You should regret it," I said. The anger in my voice surprised me. Perhaps I should have been flattered to learn that two guys had fought over me. It hurt more that neither had put up much of a fight. Or I might have simply been embarrassed to find out that the situation hadn't been what I thought. There was a mix of negative emotions clouding the fact that John might actually be telling me something I wanted to hear. I didn't want to hear it now, not when my head was full of things that might have been different if I had known. Why did he tell me now? I didn't want to know now.

"I do regret it," John said. "I have never regretted anything more." He appeared determined to tell me everything whether I was ready or not. "I should never have left it to chance. I should... *we* should have let you decide. Even if you'd turned me down, I think that would have been easier than not knowing what might have happened. I tried not to be jealous. I tried to be happy for you. But eventually I realized that I wasn't doing a good job and that you could see it. I knew you thought I hated you, not that I hated seeing you with someone else. But I couldn't tell you. As long as you were with Tyler, I couldn't confess something that would only make you uncomfortable in a different way. But now... I just can't stand the thought of you thinking I found something wrong with you when there is *nothing...*"

He closed his eyes and his Adam's apple bobbed. "You are the most beautiful person I know, inside and out. And I am so sorry for dumping this on you. I know it isn't... the timing, the situation... it's not..." He shook away those thoughts and met my eyes. I looked into the dark eyes that had been speaking to me for months and finally understood what they were saying. He loved me. "I just don't want to regret stepping back again. I have no right to ask you this, but what I'm asking is... please

~ 123 ~

just don't start dating anyone else until you've thought about me. And don't tell me *now* if you already know there's nothing to think about. This is bad enough for you without having to… I just needed to tell you. And now… well… goodnight, Heidi." He put his hand on mine and gently ran his fingers over the back of it before he pulled away again.

My fingers trembled as John turned to enter his car. And my heart hurt. It had begun beating frantically when he said I shouldn't tell him there was nothing to think about because he'd looked so sure that was what I was going to say. I wanted to stop him, to tell him that I was already thinking about him. It all just seemed so sudden though, and I didn't want to be wrong again.

14

I'd woken up to that same optical illusion poster nearly every day since sometime in middle school. One of my sister Sharon's friends gave it to her for Christmas and she hung it in the room we shared. Sharon got married when she was only nineteen, and that's when she moved out. She abandoned the poster so I took it with me when I moved out. I wanted as many familiar surroundings in my new apartment as I could carry.

I slept in on Saturday and somehow familiar wasn't quite as comforting as usual when I opened my eyes. I didn't linger in bed but moved quickly to the kitchen for breakfast. I ate fast, showered fast, began to pace my apartment. I didn't work until later in the afternoon and I was way too restless. I needed something to do with myself. I picked up my phone and thought about who to contact.

Griffin came to mind first, along with my word to his grandmother that I would try to talk to him. I was trying, but so far I was failing. I had texted him after work as planned. Repeatedly. I tried to strike up a friendly conversation without sounding so friendly that he'd think I was trying to hit on him. I sat on my couch and reviewed those texts to see if they still sounded casual in the light of a new day.

```
Hi, Griffin.  Your grandmother let me know
you made it home.  Thanks for telling me
yourself.
    No.  That last one wasn't sarcastic.  I'm
really glad you care that I was worried.
    I got to enter all my orders in peace
today.  It was so weird.
```

I'm not trying to say I missed you at work
though.
      You're not going to insist I'm lying to
myself?
      Fine. Ignore me.
      Actually, it's not fine. You could at
least let me know this is the right number.
      This is almost as stimulating as the talks
we had at work.
      Goodnight, Griffin. I can take a hint.
Eventually.

He still hadn't responded to me. I'd sent those texts every few minutes for nearly an hour. At the moment I had the sense that I shouldn't push it. I would leave Griffin alone for a while. I thought about texting Tyler.

We needed more time though. Especially if there was any chance something was going to happen between me and John. The guys should probably work that out before I talked to Tyler.

Of course I thought about John, too. I was kind of thinking about him a lot, mostly when I was trying not to think about him. I hoped I'd get a chance to say hello after church. I was starting to worry that I might not see him though. I was worried that he might be embarrassed to show up after making a big speech about being in love with the girl his best friend just broke up with because... well, was there anyone who couldn't see why that might be embarrassing?

But I couldn't do anything about possibly not seeing him the next day. Aside from possibly making a declaration of my own. I had decided to move slowly though. I was really worried that if he knew the head start my feelings had gotten, he might not trust me to be faithful. I was only going to say hello.

I needed to contact my grandparents and get myself over the fear that they weren't pestering me this time because they weren't excited. They'd never been pestering sort of people. It was even possible they hadn't mentioned the trip again because they worried *I* wasn't excited. I was the one who canceled after all. I typed: I'm off tomorrow. Can we do the
museum after lunch?

Then I decided to text Sharon.

Hi, Sis. I'm bored. You available to do
something for lunch?

I had barely finished my breakfast, but my offer of lunch was
about socializing and not food.

Sharon: Sorry. Gotta take the kids
shopping.

Me: I'm so bored I'll babysit if you want
to go alone.

Sharon: Skyler needs shoes. Need to bring
her feet.

My sister was odd. I had a picture in my head of her
carrying her daughter into the store by her feet to try shoes on
them. Maybe I couldn't blame her for the picture. Maybe I was
odd.

Granddad replied: Absolutely. We're looking
forward to it!

I smiled as I took him at his word. I actually wished I had
time to go right away. If I waited for a day off though, I could
stay with them longer.

I tried Maggie next. I knew she was working the same hours
as me later.

Are you busy before work today?

Maggie: I'm free! Do you want to do
something?

Me: Yeah. Ideas?

Maggie: No. I'm pathetic.

Me: Something outside. Now do you have an
idea?

Maggie: Bike ride?

I had a bike. My dad had found it for me at a garage sale
when I was ten. I hadn't ridden in ages though. It sounded fun.
We arranged a time and place to meet. I loaded my bike into my
car only a few minutes later. Maggie said she'd bring a tire
pump, and it looked like I'd need it. Her bike was newer and
shinier than mine. She was also wearing aerodynamic clothes
with a matching helmet. I stood in my everyday shorts and tank
top while she inflated my tires, and I felt a little like a kid trying
to swing at a major league pitch.

"When you suggested a bike ride," I said, "you didn't mean a race or a cross-country trek or…"

"No, no. Just an excuse to be outside." She looked at her outfit. "It's just that biking is my favorite type of exercise so I splurged a bit on supplies."

I wasn't sure I believed her, but I started to when she set a reasonable pace. We rode side by side on the trail when there was no one else there and had a nice chat. She told me about the classes she was registered to start in the fall. Maggie was planning to become a nurse. I had a feeling she'd be good at it. That day-brightening smile would be an asset, and she was smart, too.

She asked if I'd seen John. That was a can of worms I wasn't ready to open. I did tell her that I was in a better place and beginning to feel optimistic about my chances with him. She laughed like she knew there was something I hadn't said.

I think we rode about forty-five minutes before we circled back to our starting point. As I was about to dismount, I told her I could see why it was her favorite exercise because it was easier than real exercise. Then I choked on the words I'd just said.

Maggie laughed at me. "Having a little trouble walking?" she asked.

"Uh…" I laughed at myself. "I'm a little wobbly. Maybe this counts as exercise after all."

"It was even more fun together. We should do this again."

"All right." I unlocked my car and opened the trunk. "But I need at least a day to recover before we schedule the next one."

"Do a good stretch while you're warm," Maggie said. Her head was somewhere near her knees.

I hoisted my bike into my car before I tried to copy Maggie. I would need to be a lot warmer to bend the way she did, but the stretch did help.

"So I'll see you at work in about," I checked my watch, "three hours."

Maggie nodded and flashed her teeth at me. "Awesome."

I waved from my car as she drove from the parking lot. Then I reached for the glove box to retrieve and check my phone. There was a text from Griffin.

`I knew you thought about me in bed.`

I got out of my car again and parked myself on a bench. This might take a while. How should I reply? Did he think I was trying to flirt? Did he know what his grandmother had told me? Or what she'd asked me to do? I'd always been a people person. I don't think I'd ever felt such uncertainty over a conversation. It was almost like watching someone else's hand trembling out a reply.

`Not EVERY night.`

`Griffin: It's gonna be hard on you, not seeing me at work.`

`Me: I didn't say I missed you. You got that text about me NOT missing you, right?`

`Griffin: Amazingly. Does your phone even have the whole alphabet?`

I smiled. Griffin mocked my cheap phone several times at work, and the impersonal topic helped me relax. I sent: `This is a perfectly good phone.`

His reply described my phone with more than one word that some people would call colorful. I stopped in the middle of typing and called Griffin before I could change my mind.

"Heidi?" He sounded puzzled as he answered.

"Just thought I'd prove my phone is fine. See? It makes calls, too."

"Wow. I'm shocked." He didn't sound shocked. He sounded sarcastic.

"So I don't need a new one," I said.

"Does it play games?"

"Some."

"Any good ones?" His tone implied he wouldn't believe me no matter what I said.

"I really don't think I need to defend my phone to you."

"Isn't that why you called?"

"Maybe." I tried to sound defensive. For the moment, I wanted him to think that *was* why I called.

He didn't say anything so he might not have been fooled. That made me think I might as well try to tiptoe towards the real reason.

"I didn't know you lived with your grandparents," I said.

"I have since I was fourteen. You wanna ask me why?"

"Not if you don't want to tell me. They were pretty upset about your disappearing act."

"That's even less your business than it was theirs."

"I know, I…" I what? "Do you have a new job lined up?"

"Is that your business either?"

Time to backpedal to something light. "Would you believe I've gotten two requests to put the pirate music back on?"

"Nope. I don't believe that for a second."

"I really did, though one person only wanted to show her friends how bad it was."

"I *almost* believe that," he said. "Though anyone I told would have to take my word for it."

"Customers didn't listen to it as much as we did."

"They never looked at me like you did either, like you were too distracted by passionate daydreams to pay any attention to the so-not-cool music."

Those weren't his exact words. My vocabulary isn't as colorful so that's what I tried to hear. Either way, we were back in familiar territory. It wasn't going to get us anywhere. If we couldn't talk about him, maybe we could talk about me. "You might have imagined that. You know I was seeing someone most of the time we worked together."

"Most of the time? Did that idiot break up with you?"

Whoa! Did I just get a compliment from Griffin? He likely only wanted to call someone an idiot and didn't realize how I might take it. "No," I said. "It was a mutual decision to end it."

"Oh. Wait a minute. Is that, um…"

It sounded as though he was trying to ask if I had called because I was now available. I was strangely comforted by the panic in his voice. "Don't worry, Griffin. I know I was only ever meant to admire you from afar."

A short and snorty laugh came through the phone. "It's about time you admitted you're hot for me. Your eyes have been saying it since you were training me."

His heart didn't seem to be in that joke, and I thought he might be getting bored with the phone call. "Well, I still won't admit I miss you at work, but…" Stay in touch? Text me sometime?

"Keep telling yourself you don't miss me."

He was going to hang up. I just blurted out what I wanted to say. "Griffin, promise me you're going to talk to the guy your grandma wants you to talk to."

I heard a gasp as he burst into laughter. I didn't know if it was funny that I was worried or that I thought it was any of my business. But the sound was faint as though he had pulled the phone away from his mouth, and I thought it was weird that he wouldn't want me to know he was laughing at me. A sniff made me realize that he wasn't laughing at all. He was crying. What had I done?

I leaned over to put my head in my hands. An ant was crawling on the sidewalk by my feet. I watched it scurry along while I listened to the most onerous guy I'd ever met prove he was human. I wished my path forward was as clear as the ant's seemed to be. It marched ahead like it knew exactly what it was doing. But what should I do? I'd already pushed too hard. I couldn't take it back.

Sympathetic tears streamed down my own face. I could never stand for someone else to be sad, and this time it felt like my fault. I knew there was more to it. It still felt like my fault. *God, help me. How can I fix this? Will you fix this?*

"Griffin…" I wanted to ask if he was okay and because that struck me as the stupidest question I could ask, I said, "You're not okay."

The sniffling got a little louder, as though he'd moved the phone closer to his ear or stopped trying to cover it. He still didn't say anything.

I didn't either. I just sat there, with him but not with him. Waiting. Offering patience while his breathing steadied.

Finally, he said, "I already told her I would. Why do you care?"

He was trying to give me attitude. I chose to treat it like a real question. "I care about everyone. I can't help it."

"Sounds like a curse."

"Maybe sometimes."

We had a few more silent minutes. I wasn't sure we had anything else to say, but something told me to let the call end on his terms. I waited for a sign he was ready.

He gave an exaggerated sigh. "If you want me to come back to work, you could just say that."

I hoped we were bonding enough to be able to inject some honesty into the relationship. "Griffin, I think we both know you suck at waiting tables. If you want to come back for a meal though, I would gladly serve you. And accept your big tip."

"You think I want to eat someplace I've alienated the entire staff?"

There was genuine laughter in his words, and I laughed with him. "That's probably a good point. Bring your grandparents. No one would dare sabotage the owners' food, and I won't tell anyone which plate is yours."

"I usually hate using their connections, but I might make an exception. Only because it means so much to *you*."

"Right."

"You keep dreaming about me, Heidi. I might just show up when you least expect it."

As I put away my phone and headed for home, I marveled at the fact that if Griffin did show up at The Sleepy Crab, I really would be happy to see him. I could not have predicted that a month ago. I doubted we were destined to become great buddies, but perhaps he was turning out to be a perfectly good man after all.

15

Sacred Heart had a stained-glass window with a depiction of the Last Supper. There were a lot of pretty windows, but that one seemed to draw my eye the most. Perhaps I related well to people gathered around a table for a meal. Or perhaps I just happened to sit near it often.

I had looked up all the hymns and was staring absently at that window when someone joined me in the pew. It was a little blond girl in a pink dress that bounced with her. She had stopped walking next to me and was still bouncing as she stood looking at me.

"Heidi!" She pressed her finger to her lips right away to remind herself to whisper.

"Hi, Olivia." I looked behind her, expecting to greet Kim. It was John who was following Olivia and carrying Kate. He reached a hand out to Olivia, intending to lead her away.

She hopped onto the pew and said, "Let's sit with Heidi." Innocence dripped from her smile as she covered her mouth again.

John sucked in a breath before he mouthed, "Do you mind?"

I shook my head. Boy, did I not mind. After some sleep and reflection, I'd managed to let go of things I couldn't change and left myself with the fact that I was falling hard for a guy who'd already told me he loved me. If we were careful, we might be able to find a path to a happy ending.

I watched out of the corner of my eye as he settled the two-year-old on his lap. He was scruffier than usual as though he hadn't had a chance to shave, maybe for more than one day. I'd never seen him that way, but it looked good on him and I caught a whiff of something pleasantly spicy. This wasn't the guy I tried not to look at while he watched baseball and wished I wasn't in the room. This was the guy who wanted to be near me and looked so sweet watching his sister's kids. I was still going to take a potential relationship very slowly and carefully, but I would need to revise my plan to only say hello. The current situation raised an important question.

I leaned across Olivia to whisper to John. "Does this mean there's been a new arrival?"

"They dropped the girls with me on their way to the hospital two... almost three hours ago. I haven't gotten any news yet."

I nodded my understanding as I sat back to focus on the mass and something else I could pray for during it. Olivia grabbed a hymnal and made sure it was on the same page as mine for the opening hymn. It took her half the song and was very cute. I didn't use the book for most of the mass, but I followed along that day for the bible readings. Olivia's determination to stay on the same page as me was particularly endearing because I didn't think she could actually read any of the pages.

She took my hand as we were leaving the church. I planned to get some coffee anyway – to go – so I walked with her and John, who was carrying Kate and turning on his phone.

Olivia relayed every thought she had... about the pretty flowers, the dress another little girl was wearing and how different it was to come to church with her Uncle John. They walked instead of taking a car. She found that fascinating. I listened quietly.

"It's a boy," John said suddenly. "Guess that makes you a big sister." He gently poked Kate's tummy.

"I'm already a big sister," Olivia said. "I guess now I'm a bigger sister."

"So what did they name him and when was he born and—"

John waved the phone at me before he put it in his pocket. "Brad's text said exactly, 'It's a boy.' That's what I know."

"But that's the one thing we already knew." Brad was Kim's husband. How could he be on his third kid and still not know that a proper birth announcement included a lot more details?

John stilled his hand with the phone halfway back in his pocket. "Do you want me to ask?" he said, glancing between me and Kate as though he wasn't sure he could do that with an armload of toddler.

"No. It's okay. I'm sure we'll find out soon enough." I bit my lip at my presumptuous use of the word *we*. John and I were not a *we*. Not yet. Maybe not ever. Although the thought entered my head that Kim would likely be back at church in a week or two and a new baby would give me an excellent excuse to talk to her… when John was with her. Casual time together might be the start of something.

Olivia kept a hold on my hand as we entered the parish hall and steered me towards the donut table before she exclaimed, "Where are the donuts?"

"Um…" She was right. Something *was* missing. I'd been watching John try not to watch me, but now that Olivia had my attention I saw that there was only coffee set out. There was a guy near the table who I knew I'd seen carrying donuts at least once before. I left Olivia with John while I approached him for information.

"Excuse me," I said. "Are you in charge of donuts?"

"Not this week." His voice was gruff as though he was tired of explaining himself, and his eyes darted impatiently around the room. "I don't know if it's Jack or Dan's turn. Neither is here and neither is picking up. I can only hope one of them is ignoring his phone because he's driving, as in, driving here with donuts." The man turned away from me as soon as he finished speaking and opened his mouth towards two more people asking about donuts. I felt sorry for him. He was in for a long morning of disappointed people.

I felt a little sorry for John, too. As I came back to report what little I knew, Olivia was rattling off a stream of questions related to when she was going to get a donut and Kate just kept saying, "Where are the donuts?" as though she did not understand how anyone could lose a giant box of donuts.

"Sorry," I said. "He doesn't know anything. Are you going to wait to see if the donuts show up?"

John looked down at Olivia.

"We always have a donut after church," she said. "You said we could still have a donut."

"Come on, girls." John held a hand out to Olivia as he appeared to make a decision. "We can find a treat at my place."

"Really?" She took his hand with a curious smile. "What are we going to have instead?"

"I'm thinking."

"What are we going to have?"

"I don't know."

I began to follow John and the girls without really thinking about what I was doing. He was starting to look worried and my instinct was to see if I could help. A young woman stopped me near the door to ask about the donuts.

I shrugged at her. "It sounds like someone forgot to pick them up but might only be running late." I shrugged again. I couldn't help her, and I couldn't help John. He looked over his shoulder at me when we got outside. Something hopeful in his eyes made me flush from head to toe.

I tried to pretend I was simply headed towards my car. "Good luck," I said to him. "Maybe I'll see you again next week."

"Bye, Heidi," John said.

Olivia stopped walking. "Heidi's coming, too, right?" She turned back to me without waiting for an answer and grabbed my hand. "Come on."

"I think Heidi might have other plans for today," John said, not looking at me or Olivia.

"No, she doesn't." Olivia tugged on my hand. "Come on, Heidi. Uncle John has donuts."

"I didn't say I had donuts." John looked at Kate to make sure she understood that point, too. "I said we'd find a treat. I'm still trying to think of what I have that's sweet."

"Do you have cookies?" Olivia asked.

"I don't think so."

"Do you have cake?"

"No."

"Do you have ice cream?"

"No."

"Do you have pop-stickles?"

"Um…" John paused to contain a laugh at her pronunciation. "No."

She listed several other desserts before I realized we had passed my car and were about to cross into the parking lot for John's apartment building. My feet had apparently started moving again without my permission. John hadn't invited me to come though. I pulled my hand from Olivia's, hoping she was distracted enough that she wouldn't notice me slip away.

"Heidi?"

It was John's voice that made me turn back.

"You're welcome to come," he said.

Olivia was nodding eagerly next to him and even Kate offered me a shy smile. I couldn't think of a rational reason to say no. All three of them wanted me to come. *I* wanted me to come. I'd said a lot more than hello already, but John wasn't asking me to marry him. He wasn't even asking me out. He was letting me tag along while he babysat.

I said, "Okay."

John's apartment was on the second floor. Kate wanted to be put down when we got to the steps so she could walk up them. She held John's hand in one of hers and the railing in the other. John had a lot more patience with the slow pace than Olivia, who stomped up the stairs to the landing and stood there calling, "Hurry up. I'm already at the top. Hurry up."

The girls rushed inside as soon as John unlocked his door. I followed slowly, thinking about the one other time I'd been in his apartment. Thanksgiving. Tyler and I had eaten with his parents then stopped by John's gathering for a while. He'd hosted his parents, Kim and her family, and a friend from work who would have otherwise spent the day alone. It was a nice memory, but it was driven from my mind by the overpowering aroma of bacon.

"Mmm." I looked at John. "Did you have bacon for breakfast?"

"Last night actually." His expression was apologetic. "The smell does linger."

"I wasn't complaining. I love the smell of bacon. It makes me think of my granddad."

"Just in general or is there a –?"

~ 137 ~

"Uncle John, where's the treat? You said we were coming back for a treat."

"Right." He nodded at Olivia and moved into the kitchen, two blond children on his heels. "I have an idea."

"What is it?" Olivia asked. She watched as he pulled a toaster from the back of a cupboard. "Is it Pop Tarts?"

I laughed and John shot me a silencing look. He hated any mention of Pop Tarts. As a kid, he'd seen someone eating one at school and begged his mom for weeks to buy some. When she finally caved, he found out that they didn't taste nearly as good as he'd hoped. His mom had never let him forget it. He claimed that for years he couldn't express an opinion, good or bad, without her saying something to the effect of, "Are you sure? You thought you loved Pop Tarts."

Olivia was still sprinkling him with questions while he got out some bread and popped two slices into the toaster.

"Why don't we watch," I said to her, "and see if we can guess what he's making?"

John's place was larger than mine but had no more furnishings so it felt very open. There were Christmas cards on the refrigerator displaying the only pictures in sight. He got out some cinnamon and some sugar, which gave me a pretty good idea what he had in mind. Olivia stared at him with her brow furrowed. Kate was trying to push a chair from the table in the next room. John would probably be done by the time she made it, but it was keeping her busy for the moment.

The bread jumped from the toaster and John flipped both slices around and pushed them down again.

"Why are you cooking it twice?" Olivia said.

"The filaments... the things that get hot don't work in the middle so you have to toast it twice to get both sides."

Olivia nodded at him very seriously, as though he was giving her important directions that she was committing to memory.

"I don't use it that often," John said, "so it isn't a big deal to flip the bread." He turned away to grab a couple plates and conceal a tiny smile. He was likely thinking that I was the last person to whom he needed to justify that toaster.

He buttered the bread and sprinkled it with cinnamon and sugar, then he set the plates on the table and helped Kate bring

~ 138 ~

her chair back. He poured two cups of coffee and two cups of milk. I carried one of each to the table and he brought the others. Olivia was nearly halfway through her toast when I set the milk in front of her.

"So it's good?" I asked.

She nodded at me with her mouth full and her eyes wide.

"I like it," Kate said.

John sighed with exaggerated relief over a sip of coffee. He turned to me. "What is it about bacon that makes you think of your grandfather?"

"Oh, yeah." I didn't really smell the bacon anymore now that we'd been inside for a while and forgot I'd mentioned it. The cinnamon and coffee had taken over and those were nice scents, too. "We used to stay with my grandparents for a weekend every now and then and we spent about a week with them whenever Mom had a new baby. This one time – I was in middle school so I think it was when Macy was born – I got back from school and asked Granddad for a snack. Sharon was there, but Grandma had taken Michael somewhere and the others were still in school because the elementary school got out later. We looked in the fridge and I saw a package of bacon and asked if we could eat that. I still remember he said, 'I don't see why not.'"

I smiled to myself, almost forgetting anyone was watching me tell the story. "Granddad fried it up and Sharon and I pigged out. In a family size, when someone fries a package of bacon, you're usually lucky to get a second piece so we were a little greedy. At the time, I was thinking we'd just eat the evidence and no one would know what they missed. Grandma came back with everyone else – she'd picked them up from school – and they *smelled* the bacon. They came in asking for bacon. I think they smelled it before they even got in the house. Granddad said it was all gone without saying that Sharon and I had actually been the ones to eat most of it. I think they assumed he'd eaten it all before we got out of school, too. That diffused what might have been a tense situation. But Grandma knew what had happened. After everyone else had left the kitchen, she said, 'Really, Chuck? Bacon was the best you could think of for an after school snack?'

He nodded at her. Then he turned and winked at me. I'm not sure I can describe what was so special about that moment but…" I refocused on my audience and made eye contact with John while I tried to describe it. "I never felt overlooked in a big family. I truly didn't. But there was still something about that one-on-one understanding that seemed to pass between us that… It felt like me and Granddad against the world for one moment, and I still see him winking at me whenever I smell bacon."

John did have the darkest eyes of anyone I knew. I could see his kitchen light reflected in the surface and beneath that was an intensity I wasn't ready for. When I broke the connection, he jumped up to help Olivia at the sink before she wiped her greasy fingers on everything. He cleared her plate and she walked over to a shelf and brought Princess Candy Land to the table. She proceeded to set it up as though John and I were as excited to play as she was.

I didn't mind and John didn't seem to mind. Kate joined his team when she finished eating and they won so we had to play again. Fortunately, Olivia won the second game. John also had a huge tub of Legos that he'd saved from when he was a kid. He said he'd only been getting them out for Olivia for a few months – since Kate no longer put everything in her mouth – and that he hadn't played with them for at least ten years previously.

I teased that his math meant he'd been playing with them in high school. He pointed out that he'd said *at least* ten years, which could mean a lot of different numbers. Given that we were having as much fun with them as the girls, under the guise of assisting them, my taunting was pretty half-hearted.

A loud knock startled all four of us from the fun. John said, "I wonder who that could be," to the girls in a way that made me think he knew.

He opened the door and both girls yelled, "Daddy!" as Brad walked in.

"Who wants to see a picture of the new baby?" he said.

I definitely wanted to see, but he was clearly talking to his daughters so I didn't join their chants of, "Me, me, me!"

Brad knelt on the floor with his phone in front of the girls while he scrolled through several pictures of a tiny burrito newborn in a bassinet and several more of him in Kim's arms. John and I peeked at the display over the girls' shoulders.

"His name is Ronan," Brad said, pride in his voice. "He and Mommy are going to rest up at the hospital, and we'll go pick them up tomorrow."

John handed Brad a bag from I had no idea where. The guys exchanged congratulations for gratitude and Brad and his girls left amidst a chorus of farewells before I understood what was happening.

What was happening was me finding myself in a still apartment with John Myrie and no warning. We were both standing there in quiet uncertainty. He was closer to the door because he'd just shown his brother-in-law through it. Neither of us moved, but it felt as though the door got closer and John got closer as everything seemed smaller with just the two of us. What had been an innocent cup of coffee now felt like me intruding in John's life.

"I, uh, should probably go, too," I said, glancing around for my purse. I'd made myself so comfortable I wasn't sure where I'd set it down. "I'm headed to see my grandparents this afternoon."

"Heidi?"

I looked at John, at his chest and not his face. It wasn't my short stature that kept me from looking higher.

"I assumed you'd avoid me like the plague after... now that, uh..."

I tried to look up. John had stepped closer though. My eyes traced the intersecting stripes in the plaid of his shirt.

"Olivia is cute," he said, "but I know you could have made any number of excuses not to come with us."

"I don't think I need to avoid you."

"Because you don't want to be rude or because you don't care how much you get my hopes up?"

I glanced up and John was looking back with so much anticipation flaring in his eyes that I knew my resolution to take the relationship slowly was about to be tested.

"I talked to Tyler," he said.

"About... me?"

He sort of shrugged. "He said, 'You like Heidi, don't you?' I said, 'Yeah.' He said, 'Try not to rub my nose in it.' I said, 'Okay.' So we're good."

I thought about Griffin's grandmother saying that guys didn't know how to talk and a nervous laugh tried to force its way from my mouth. I swallowed it. "I have been thinking about... well, I thought... I thought we could try to spend a little time as friends to see... you know, for a while."

"Friends," he said. "For a while?" He didn't sound disappointed. It looked as though he understood my implication that a temporary friendship could give way to something better.

I didn't know what else to say. We'd established possibilities and boundaries and now what? There was chemistry between us and around us and pulsing right through me and I was letting myself admit how long it had been there. How could we go from an intense moment of understanding mutual desire back to a casual relationship?

"Would you, um... like a rematch at Princess Candy Land?" I suggested lamely. I reached out to take John's hand, intending a gentle tug towards an innocent toy. His skin was hot, and I didn't tug so much as squeeze.

His other hand found its way into my hair. My eyelids dropped at the touch – slowly – but this wasn't the kind of slowly we were supposed to be following.

"I don't need a rematch," he said. "I won, remember?"

I opened my eyes just enough that I wasn't surprised by the feel of John's lips on mine. He kissed me slowly, too. Slowly, deeply, with enough controlled passion that I wanted to forget everything except him. But I didn't. I let myself enjoy the kiss only while my fingers crept up the front of his shirt. Then I used my arms to separate us.

"I'm sorry," John said. He shook his head. "No, no... I'm not sorry at all. I wanted to do that for way too long." He clasped my hands in his and put them down between us. "But I promise to behave myself now. For a while." He stepped back and let go of my hands. "So you need to go?"

"I..." Did I really need to go? Maybe he could kiss me a few more times and then we could try to be friends. I shook my head at myself.

"You don't?" John moved a little closer again.

I smiled as I took hold of his hand and settled my thoughts. "I do have to go. I planned to eat a little early so I could get to my grandparents' place right after they finish lunch."

"There's food *here*. What can I make that will entice you to stay?"

"I'm not hungry. Not really."

John wrinkled his eyes at me and his confusion only made the offer to stay more tempting.

"Look. I don't think we're doing the just friends thing right." My fingers were caressing his hand as I spoke. "I need to go now so we can cool off and try again some other time."

He laughed heartily as he pulled his hand from mine. Then he handed me my purse. I thanked him for the coffee, and he thanked me for helping him entertain his nieces. We did a good job of pretending that was what we were thinking about as I left.

I hadn't even started my car when I got a text from John. When exactly is some other time?

I smiled at his impatience and typed out: I'm not working until late tomorrow. Meet me at The Sleepy Crab for lunch?

Maggie would be there. We could ask for her. Perhaps meeting the very next day didn't show a lot of patience on my part either. It was the next day though and that's how I intended to take the relationship… one day at a time. I hadn't made any decisions yet, but I was beginning to think John Myrie could end up as something good in my life. Something truly and perfectly good.

~~ The End ~~

Thanks for reading.

www.ingramcontent.com/pod-product-compliance
Lightning Source LLC
Chambersburg PA
CBHW030614130626
46552CB00002B/567